AF270136

BACK IN BLACK

BACK IN BLACK

AN ANTHOLOGY OF NEW MYSTERY SHORT STORIES BY

REED FARREL COLEMAN • HEATHER GRAHAM • ANDREW CHILD
DON BRUNS • SANDRA BALZO • RICK BLEIWEISS • DAVE BRUNS
CHARLES TODD • TORI ELDRIDGE • WARD LARSEN

EDITED BY DON BRUNS

BLACK STONE PUBLISHING

First edition: 2024
ISBN 979-8-200-92463-9
Fiction / Mystery & Detective / Collections & Anthologies

Version 1

Blackstone Publishing
31 Mistletoe Rd.
Ashland, OR 97520

www.BlackstonePublishing.com

TABLE OF CONTENTS

RICK BLEIWEISS

SHAKE A LEG

CHAPTER ONE

The Hawaiian summer day was blisteringly hot. Well over 90 degrees. The cloudless sky was filled with a giant ball of sun that beat down unmercifully. Humidity hung in the air like a shroud, and sweat dripped from every pore on his now glistening muscular body as he ran bare-chested and barefooted across the open field. The flowers and grass partially cushioned his tired, sore feet as stones and twigs poked him with unseen barbs and small daggerlike protrusions.

Despite running for more than an hour, he still ran fast. The years of marathons and physical training seemed to him to have been part of some plan to prepare him for just this. He swore he could feel the adrenaline coursing through his body, in a seemingly never-ending supply, propelling him onward at a torrid nonstop pace. He was sure he had outrun everyone and everything, but still, he kept looking over his shoulder every few minutes. Occasionally he heard sounds behind him in the distance, and each time he would summon up the strength to run just a little faster while he exhorted himself to "shake a leg."

He didn't know exactly from whom he was running. He had absolutely no idea where he was running. No idea what he would do once he got to a *someplace else*. He did know that he wanted there to be a stream somewhere ahead. He could momentarily stop and cool down in it. And he needed to drink. He craved water. His mouth was parched, his body ached, and he had lost so much fluid from the sweat flying off him that he swore he could hear every cell in his body crying out for life-sustaining liquid.

The field was bigger than it originally looked. When he entered it from the grove of palm trees on its eastern edge, he thought it would take a reasonably short sprint to cross it. He was wrong. He had been traversing it for an hour already. It had sloped down and continued in a way that he couldn't have seen from the trees. He had been concerned about being in the open, but so far, he had seen no other living creatures except for an occasional bird or feral rabbit.

A shot rang out.

It startled him. Made him momentarily falter.

Another shot.

He ran. He zigzagged. He listened.

Another shot.

He ran a little bit faster, and as he sprinted, he listened intently for the next shot. When it came, he realized that the sounds were off to his right. Down by the northern hills that bordered the farthest edge of the field. One that he was running parallel to.

He kept running, now ignoring the sounds of the gun or rifle fire that continued for the next five minutes. He hoped they were hunters trying to bring down some animal bigger than any he had seen that day, but he knew they might just be practicing before coming at him with their weapons.

As he continued to run, he thought about many things—his wife, his life, the career that now was over, and the people he worked and played with. He wondered if he would see any of them again, or if anything would ever be the same. Sometimes he sang songs. But they never crossed his parched lips, only playing in the jukebox of his mind.

And then, out of nowhere, he found himself yelling. Very loudly. Screaming out the first words he had spoken aloud since he began running.

"WHAT HAVE I DONE?"

And then in quiet desperation, he muttered, "What *have* I done?"

Before he could find an answer, or even contemplate one, he saw the end of the field. It came up sooner than he had dared to hope. The enormous group of looming trees now looked to be less than a five-minute run. He urged his body to give him strength and summoned up all the internal reserves he could muster. He pumped and ran, pumped and ran, pumped and ran.

He hoped he could reach the trees before anyone saw him or anyone else entered the field.

He heard a new sound in the distance. He ran. It got louder and louder. He ran slower and slower. His body was giving out. His heart was pumping faster than his legs. The trees were getting closer but still seemed far away. The sound too was still far away but getting closer. He slowed, almost walking, and listened. What *was* the sound? He knew it but couldn't place it. And then he recognized it. It was the loud engine of a Hummer, a truck, or a large ATV. He heard it before he saw it, but now it was starting to crest the ridge like a metallic predator from the hills where he had heard the shots.

He knew he had to make the trees. He had to reach them before the people in the vehicle saw him. But could he?

He asked a god he wasn't sure he believed in for the strength to reach the safety of the trees. He walked a little faster. He hurt everywhere. His eyes were red and raw, and he was almost blinded from the ever-present perspiration that he was constantly wiping away. His legs throbbed and his feet bled.

The trees were getting closer, but the truck was advancing toward him quickly. And he could see a shotgun protruding from the front passenger's window. It was a race. He wondered if it was a race to the finish.

He ran, he trotted, he walked.

And he won.

He reached the tree line. He ran between two koa trees and into the dense coolness of the large grove. He didn't notice the harsher tearing at his feet by the grassless floor beneath him. He was too tired and too overjoyed at having reached cover. He slowed to the walk of an invalid, but kept on, going deeper and deeper into the grouping of trees, hoping to find water and food.

The police search that his wife asked for was called off after a week. Most people forgot about the incident once the newspapers stopped reporting on the man who disappeared.

CHAPTER TWO

The former premier New York City hitman—who called himself Walker—remained in Maui after an attempt on *his* life failed, and he later took out the second assassin sent after him to finish the job. Shortly after recovering from that cat-and-mouse game, he got caught up in saving a teenage girl from a Hawaiian gang who had killed her parents and then come after her. Since neither he nor the girl, Sarah, had any close relatives—and with her still being hunted by the gang—she and Walker struck an arrangement for him to become her guardian. He got them both new identities, she dyed and cut her hair, and together they ensured that who they used to be disappeared. To each other, they were Walker and Sarah, but to the rest of the world, he was Fred Harding and she Sarah Harding.

After Walker killed the gang members who were sent after her, he and Sarah stayed at the Oceanview Resort in South Kihei for two weeks until things cooled down and the killing of her parents, and the search for her, were no longer major news stories. During that time, Walker asked Sarah where she thought they should live. He didn't think it was safe for either of them to remain in Kihei.

Sarah suggested, "What about Hana? It's kind of remote and on the other side of the island. Mom and Dad took me there a couple of times, and I liked it. And I know they have a high school."

Walker shrugged. "Sounds like it's as good as anyplace else. Let's check it out."

The next day, to Sarah's delight, Walker purchased a black BMW convertible, with cash, which they used to take a trip to Hana to look for somewhere to live. On only the second day of going in and out of homes, they both fell in love with a house that sat right on the beach. It was vacant and fully furnished, and—because Walker paid in cash—they were able to move in within two weeks. Once they were settled, Walker arranged with his underworld friend in New York, Junior, to have school records created so that Sarah Harding would appear to be transferring from Stuyvesant High School in New York.

Sitting on lounge chairs on the house's rear deck, Walker looked away from the ocean and turned to Sarah. "You'll start school next Monday. Nervous?"

Sarah answered, "A little."

Walker waved his hand at her. "You'll be fine. You're bright and cute. You'll fit right in. But that's next week. Right now, let's focus on tonight. What should we have for dinner?"

Sarah flipped up her sunglasses and looked at him. "I can cook if you want."

Walker shook his head. "Nah. Don't get me wrong, I consider myself very lucky that you cook as well as you do, but let's go out tonight. I understand that Huli Huli Chicken is really good."

Sarah responded, "Yum. You're not gonna get an argument from me," and put her sunglasses back down.

Walker turned back toward the ocean and took a sip of the Cristom Pinot Noir he was nursing. "I'm gonna get started on that service to help people who need assistance or protection I've been talking about since we met. I've got a pretty good idea how to do it. I'll put an ad in the newspaper and online and run it every day."

Sarah asked, "And what'll it say?"

He answered, "I haven't got it fully figured out yet, but I think it'll be something like this: *Need Help? If someone's causing you trouble you don't know how to deal with, then you need the White Knight. I'll be your knight in shining armor and handle any problem you have, no matter how big or small. Everything taken care of discreetly and effectively. Contact me. Results guaranteed.*"

He continued, "And I'll list a phone number and an email address. What d'ya think?"

Sarah smiled. "I like it. Especially the knight-in-shining-armor part."

Walker nodded. "Thought you would."

"You gonna have an office?" Sarah asked.

Walker knew he needed to make it as hard as possible for anyone from New York who might be sent to find him, but he didn't want to tell Sarah that because he knew it would scare her. "Nope. If people need me, I'll go to *them*. I'm goin' to stay anonymous. I don't need any local cops breathin' down my neck. So no one gets a name. Just *the White Knight*. No way I want anyone to know about you or my personal life."

Sarah asked, "Can't they find you from your phone? Doesn't it track you everywhere you go?"

Walker drained his wine and put the glass on the deck. "Believe me, kid, I know how to disable all that. No one is findin' me unless I *want* them to. I'll get a phone just for the White Knight stuff."

Sarah turned to face the ocean. "I've got a question. Why're you gonna do *anything*? You seem to have more money than I ever thought possible."

Walker thought about how he wanted to answer her as he picked up his glass and poured more wine into it until it was half full. "I like the action. I'm lookin' forward to it. I'd be bored out of my mind if I just sat around all day. My whole life's been about gettin' rid of bad people. First overseas in the Marines and then in New York. I guess it's just ingrained in me. It's who I am and what I do."

Sarah took a sip from the water bottle sitting on the deck next to her chair. "And for the government. You *are* a marshal."

Walker recoiled slightly from his oversight. He had shown her the fake credentials he had taken off the body of the hit person he took out and had adapted to make it look like he was a marshal. "Oh yeah. And for the feds. Changin' the subject, kid, how about we take a drive into Kahului and go shoppin' before dinner? I can get that phone, and we can buy you a new one too, a computer, and some more clothes for school. I want my kid to be the best-dressed one there."

He turned to look at Sarah and saw a tear running down her cheek from under her sunglasses. "You okay?"

Sarah lifted up the glasses and wiped the tear away. "I'm so grateful for you, Walker, but I miss my parents. And my friends."

"I get it, kid," Walker acknowledged. "I can't imagine how hard it is, but your whole life's in front of you, and I'm goin' to make sure it's as great as it can be. You got that?"

"I do," Sarah sobbed. "But I still miss them."

"Makes me feel kind of helpless. I don't know what to do to make you feel better," Walker confided.

"Me either," Sarah said. "It's still so new to me."

Walker stood up. "Let's drown those tears with some cool shoppin'. We'll hit the chicken place on the way back."

CHAPTER THREE

In New York, at the same time Sarah started school in Hana, Junior's friend Cindy created a White Knight website and had it up and running within a week. Once it was functional, Walker placed an advertisement for his White Knight service in the print and online versions of the *Maui News* and *Maui Time* and paid for it to run in every edition they published for four weeks.

Sitting at dinner the following week, he told Sarah, "I'll expand it to papers on other islands after a while, but first I want to try it out here. Since I'm payin' cash, I'll have to travel to pay for the other placements."

Sarah took a bite of her mahi-mahi. "Can't you just get a credit card?"

Walker took a sip of his pinot. "You know, I probably can. Good idea. I'll have Junior get me one. Thanks for suggestin' it. How's school goin'?"

Sarah looked up from her plate. "Okay. I met this girl, Kalena, and I think we'll be friends. We might meet up for a movie this weekend."

Walker smiled. "That's good. I'll drop you off there."

"Actually," Sarah responded, "she's a grade ahead of me and has a car. Listen, Walker, I can get a permit. Wanna teach me how to drive?"

Walker took a gulp of his wine. "Whoa. I didn't think of that. Sure. But I guess there's another car in our future, huh?"

"For sure."

It only took three days after the ad ran before Walker got a call on his White Knight phone.

"Hello," the voice said, "is this the White Knight?"

"It is," Walker responded. "How can I help you?"

The female voice asked, "Can you really help with anything?"

"I can," Walker reported. "Tell me what your problem is."

The woman hesitatingly responded, "My husband disappeared. He went out for a run and never came back. The police have stopped looking for him, and I can't go on not knowing if he's alive or dead. Also, two men who claim they're from his office have been coming to my house at least twice every week since he went missing. They keep asking me if I've heard from Dave. That's my husband's name. Earlier today, when I told them I still haven't, they said they'd be back later this week because Dave owed his employer a lot of money. And they said that wasn't a good thing for me. They scared the bejesus out of me today the way they looked and were acting. Can you help me? Can you find Dave?"

Walker answered, "I probably can. Now, let's start with your name."

"I'm Amanda. Amanda Peters."

"And where do you live, Amanda Peters?" Walker asked.

"Happy Valley."

Walker winced. "It doesn't sound like Happy Valley's too happy these days."

"It's a shitty place to live, but it's where Dave and I grew up," Amanda replied.

"Where exactly is it located? I'm new to the island."

Amanda answered, "Not too far from the airport."

"And when did Dave disappear?"

"Three weeks ago," Amanda responded.

"Do you know why he went off the grid?" Walker asked.

"Dave told me he had a situation at work but didn't say exactly what it was. He only said it had to do with a lot of missing money."

Walker thought for a moment before continuing. "Where'd he work, Amanda?"

"At an investment firm, Harley Rose and Associates," she said. Then she asked, "Are you sure you can find him?"

Walker didn't hesitate. "Here's what I want you to do. Go to my website and upload pictures of you and Dave. And fill out the part that asks what happened with as many details as you can. Will you do that today?"

"Yes," Amanda confirmed.

"Good. If you do that now, then you and I can meet tomorrow mornin' and I can get started."

Amanda responded, "I work at Maui Honda, and I'm supposed to be there tomorrow, but I'll take the morning off."

Walker sternly said, "You do need to do that. Meet me at nine at the Burger King in the Departures terminal at the airport."

"At the airport?" Amanda asked, surprised.

"Yeah," Walker answered. "It's near you, open and public. Just in case you're being watched."

"How will I recognize you?"

Walker answered, "I'll find *you*—from the photos you upload. Can I count on you being there?"

Amanda answered, "I'll be there. But how much'll this cost? We don't have a lot of money."

Walker laughed. "I thought you'd get around to askin' that. Don't worry. You'll be able to afford it. I might even do this one for free."

"Are you for real?"

Walker stated firmly, before disconnecting the call, "I am. Believe it. See you tomorrow at nine."

As soon as the line went dead, Walker dialed New York.

"I need a favor, Junior."

"Anything, Walker. What is it?"

"Find out anythin' you can about Harley Rose and Associates and a former employee of theirs, Dave Peters. Both of them are on Maui. I need the info ASAP. Today—or rather, where you are—tonight?"

"Can't promise the speed, but I'll get started on it right away," Junior confirmed.

Walker smiled. "You're a good friend, guy. Thanks." Then he hung up the phone.

CHAPTER FOUR

At six fifteen the next morning, Walker was awakened by his ringing cell phone. He picked it up and yawned as the line connected. "Yeah?"

The sound of Junior's familiar voice came through the device. "That you, Walker?"

"It is," he slurred. "Sorry. I musta been unintelligible. When I answered, my mouth was cavernously open from being jolted out of a most pleasant dream, replete with scantily clad young dancin' women in a posh New York club."

Junior laughed. "Damn. Sorry to have interrupted that, but I have the info you asked me to get."

"That's great, fill me in."

"It seems that Harley Rose does handle investments, but mostly for the Hawaiian Mob and some of their gangs. He did that in Chitown but suddenly left one day under somewhat suspicious circumstances. Apparently there, and now on Maui, his associates are a combination of goons and financial guys who know how to make illegitimate money disappear legitimately. Dave Peters was one of the latter—a financial guy. I was told he didn't know what was going on until shortly before he took it on the run."

"Is there anythin' else?"

"Yep," Junior confirmed. "The day Peters disappeared, Rose told one of his goons that over three mil was missing from two of his biggest unsavory clients' accounts. Rose told him to go after Peters, saying he believed Peters embezzled the money."

Walker scratched his head. "Did they find him? Or the money?"

"Nope and nope. They're still looking for him, and since Rose could be in deep shit with his clients, he's turned up the heat. Especially on Peters's wife, Amanda, who he thinks knows where her hubby and the money are."

Walker arched his back and stretched his arms out wide before responding. "Junior, his wife contacted me and asked if I'd help find him. I really don't think she knows where he or that payload are. I'm not sure she even knows he supposedly pilfered the cash."

"Then you'd better find Peters and the dough before Rose has his guys do something really bad to her. But I did have another thought, Walker."

"Tell me."

"I wouldn't put it past Rose to have siphoned off the money himself and then blamed it on Peters when Peters discovered it."

Walker broke in, "Makes sense to me. And if that's the case, then Rose wants Peters dead before he can say anythin' to anyone."

"Bam!" Junior yelled into his cell. "Got that right."

Walker's body stiffened at the thought of that possibility. "I'd better go meet Peters's wife and then drop in on this Harley Rose. I have a way of rootin' out the truth."

"I'll bet you do," Junior confirmed, before adding, "If I learn anything else, I'll ring you up."

"Thanks, but I think you've already given me most of what I need to know for now. But one thing: How'd you learn all that?"

Junior laughed. "You know better than to ask that, Walker. I got insiders everywhere."

"You do," Walker agreed. "And I'm surely glad for it."

After showering and dressing, Walker waved goodbye to Sarah as she headed off to school with her friend Kalena. Then he went to his computer and studied the information and photos Amanda had uploaded to his website.

After he finished, he poured a cup of coffee from the still-warm pot Sarah had made earlier, toasted a bagel, smeared it high with Philadelphia cream cheese and sat down to read the news on his iPad. Once he was done, he cleared the dishes into the sink and then headed out to the airport Burger King.

When he got there, Walker surveyed the people sitting at the tables in the food court, looking for the slightly overweight, neither attractive nor unattractive, somewhat-short-haired, late-thirtysomething redhead who was in the pictures Amanda had posted. When he didn't see her among any of the diners, he shifted his gaze to those standing near the counter and almost immediately spied Amanda by the trash bin, nervously tapping her foot and curling a loose strand of crimson hair between her fingers.

He quickly approached her and forced a large smile, hoping to calm her down. "Amanda?"

Her eyes widened.

"I'm your White Knight. Shall we sit down and talk?"

Amanda nodded silently and obediently followed Walker to a table as far from the counter and the other diners as possible.

Once seated, Walker started right in. "I've read everything you put on my website—and thank you for the completeness of it—but I still don't understand one thin'. Regardin' the three million that's disappeared. You know about that, right?"

Amanda nodded slowly.

"Did your husband steal it, or did he uncover that it was missin'? If it's the former, I need to find him to recover the money and keep you safe. But if it's the latter, it would have been his boss, or someone else at Harley Rose, who pilfered it, and I need to take care of them."

Amanda leaned across the table and looked Walker squarely in the eye. "I know my Dave, and he would *not* have taken that money. If he did, he would've told me.

"Just before he went out to run, he said something happened at work, and he was afraid some really bad people would be coming after him. I asked if he stole anything, and he swore he didn't. I believe my husband," she added.

Walker leaned back and contemplated Amanda's statements for a few seconds before he moved closer to the table and put his left arm on it. "I'll find out, but I do tend to believe your husband and what you think happened. Bad people do bad things, and from what I've learned, Harley Rose is a bad person."

Amanda tilted her head, and her body visibly tightened before she responded, "Do you think you can find Dave and help us so he's not in danger?"

"I do, for sure. Count on it, Amanda," Walker replied with an assurance in his voice that made Amanda's body relax. "I'm goin' to have a meetin' with Mr. Harley Rose and make him a bit uncomfortable. Then we'll see what happens from there."

Amanda placed her hand on Walker's arm. "Thank you so much."

Walker slid his arm back and stood up. "I'll start workin' on it right away, and if those thugs come back, you call me the second you see them. I don't think you're ever goin' to be bothered by them again, but they might be stupid enough to not take me seriously. I'll be in touch. Probably tomorrow. Maybe even later today."

Walker left Amanda sitting at the table, went to his car, and drove out of the airport.

As he did, he called Junior, explained the situation, and then Junior related what he had further learned about Harley Rose and his associates. "I confirmed with another of my sources that he indeed launders for a few local gangs and the island's top organized crime guys. He's the pass-through who washes the dirty money and makes it clean. He has full access to everything since he's each one's accountant as well. Pretty good setup for Mr. Harley Rose, I'd say. Bet he rakes in a fortune."

"Probably does," Walker agreed. "But probably got greedy too. And I'll bet Dave Peters discovered that and went to Rose and told him the money was missin', not knowin' Rose was the one who embezzled it."

Junior added, "And that means Rose would have wanted to shut him up before Peters told anyone else and word of it got out."

"That's my guess too," Walker confirmed. "Rose wouldn't want the gangs he took it from to know he stole from them. He'd be deader than Dave Peters, and way faster if they found out. And that's my leverage."

Walker paused. "But there's still the outside chance that Peters did take the money. And Rose is innocent—at least of doing that."

Junior nodded a nod that Walker could hear through the phone. "You're right. Could be either. But I'd bet on Rose embezzling it. Need anything else from me?"

Walker turned left off the airport road before responding. "Nope. Not about that. But keep your ears open and let me know if you hear anythin' about the guys back there who set me up. I don't want any visitors here while I'm trying to get this thin' done. Capisce?"

Junior replied, "Capisce," before ending the call.

Walker made a right turn toward Harley Rose's office.

CHAPTER FIVE

When Walker parked his car in a spot marked Reserved for Manny Laguna, he noticed that the car next to him, a brand-new-looking red Mercedes two-seater convertible, was sitting in front of a sign that said Reserved for Harley Rose.

Walker muttered, "I guess the man is in. And he appears to have expensive taste. Then again, if he did take the money, he could've bought a Lamborghini."

Walker got out of his car and briskly strode toward the one-story, light blue octagonal building sitting adjacent to the lot. When he reached it, he opened and walked through the glass front door engraved with large white letters, Harley Rose & Associates, Accounting and Financial Planning, and in smaller letters below: Harley Rose, Financial Planner, and Manny Laguna, CPA.

The twentysomething bronzed, blond receptionist sitting behind the front counter looked to Walker as though she would be more at home on a surfboard than in an office. She looked up and took her earbuds out when he reached her. "Can I help you?"

Instead of answering, Walker casually asked, "Listenin' to somethin' good?"

The blond responded, "Yeah. Pink. I just love her. Are you here for financial services?"

Walker took the counterfeit US Marshal's credentials out of his pants pocket and held it up toward her. "Nope. Not about financial help. Marshal Fred Hardin' here. I'd like to speak with Mr. Harley Rose, please. Is he in?"

The girl's eyes widened. "Did he do something?"

Walker chuckled. "Well, sweetheart, I can't rightfully answer that without knowin' him and what he does, can I?" Walker hesitated before continuing to lie to her. "But if you're askin' if I'm here because of somethin' Mr. Rose has done, I'm not. I need to ask him about a man I'm trackin'. A Dave Peters."

The girl nodded. "I knew Dave. He was a nice guy. And a hard worker. And then one day a few weeks ago he just didn't show up for work, and after that I saw the news that he ran away, and the police couldn't find him."

"That's exactly why I'm here. Trust me, sweetheart, I *will* find him. Now why don't you buzz Mr. Rose and get me a few minutes of his time."

The girl picked up the phone, hit an intercom button, and almost as quickly as she hung it up and put her earbuds back in place, the door to the front office to the left of the counter opened.

A fit-looking older man sporting a manicured salt-and-pepper mustache, dressed in what Walker assessed to be quite expensive uncreased tan linen slacks and a floral Hawaiian shirt, confidently walked up to him. "May I see your credentials?"

Walker replied, "Of course," and handed his marshal's wallet to the man.

After he inspected the ID, the man handed it back to Walker. "I'm Harley Rose. Shall we go into my office and discuss Dave Peters? I believe you said he's the fugitive you're looking for."

Walker motioned his head slightly toward the door Rose had come out of. "Yes, let's talk in there."

Rose led Walker to his office and closed the door behind them.

When he did, Walker leisurely ambled to the blinds hanging above the three large windows, lowered the shades, and closed the slats.

Standing with his hands on his hips next to his elegantly carved mango-wood desk, Rose asked, "What are you doing?"

Walker shuttered the last blind and lied, "The sunlight hurts my eyes. I prefer indoor lightin'."

Satisfied with the unusual but seemingly rational explanation, given the intensity of the sun, Rose motioned Walker to the couch and sat down on the lounge chair facing it. "You sound like you're from New York."

Walker nodded. "Got that right. Born and bred."

Rose shifted on the chair. "Now what's this all about with Dave Peters?"

Walker casually leaned back, crossed his left leg over his right at the knee, and let his hands fall to his lap—positions he purposefully took to relax Rose and take him off his guard. "I'm after the man for theft. No more, no less."

That piqued Rose's interest. "What kind of theft?"

"Financial," Walker lied, and then added sarcastically, "What other type of theft would you think someone like Peters would be capable of? Robbing a bank?"

Rose quickly fell into the trap Walker was setting, realizing that if Peters had stolen before it would make his current story more credible, so he played along. "Sorry. You're right. That was stupid of me. You know he stole from me too, only I haven't reported it because I can't prove it yet."

Walker faked ignorance. "He did?"

Rose nodded and explained. "I trusted Dave, but now with you here telling me he's stolen before, maybe that was stupid of me. I recently let him handle the books for a few of my biggest accounts, and between two of them, I've discovered over three million dollars is missing. I still can't believe he'd have taken that money, or even how he'd have pulled it off, but it's gone. Vanished."

Walker let a tiny smirk escape from his lips. "I imagine that's not gone over well with your clients."

Rose put his hand up, like a crossing guard stopping cars. "I haven't told them yet. Until I find Peters and get that money back, I'm not saying anything to anyone. I don't need that aggravation. In fact, other than a couple of my most trusted longtime employees, only you know anything about it."

Walker tugged on his earlobe. "What if it wasn't Peters? Couldn't it have been one of your other guys?"

Rose shook his head. "Nah. Not really. Only me, Peters, and Manny had access to the accounts, and Manny's my *hoaloha*. He's been with me since before I started this firm. We're like brothers. And he's been out of the country starting up our new office in Mexico for the past year. Nope, it had to be Peters who stole the money."

Walker laughed. "Despite your reasoning, Harley, that sounds like a SLOG to me."

"A *SLOG*? What the hell is a SLOG?"

"A shit load of garbage," Walker derisively explained. "What you just said—that truly does seem like it could be a shit load of garbage. A SLOG." Walker let out a broader smile. "You see, if we discount Manny, that leaves Peters and you as the only people who had access to the accounts and their ledger books. And how would Peters have actually taken it? I'll bet only you and this Manny had access to the actual accounts."

Rose shot up from the chair and glared at Walker. The tone in his voice was unmistakably confrontational. "If you're intimating that I had anything to do with that money's disappearance, you can get out of here right now. Marshal or no marshal."

Walker slowly rose from the couch until he was standing at his maximum height, rising at least three inches over Rose. He took two short steps, put his face right up to Rose's, and growled, "You don't tell me what to do or not to do. You got that, Harley Rose? In my mind, you're just as likely to have embezzled that money as Peters is to have stolen it. In fact, I'd put money on you being the one who made that money disappear—and when Peters discovered it in the books he was working on, he came to you to report it being gone. Now, you couldn't have him blabbin', could you, because the people it belongs to aren't very nice, and you wouldn't want them findin' out. So you had to get rid of Peters to shut him up. But he beat you to it by takin' it on the lam before you could do anythin'."

Rose ran to his desk, opened the top drawer, and reached for his pistol. But Walker was right behind him and as Rose started to lift the gun, Walker swatted it out of his hand, sending it clanking to the floor. In the same motion, Walker grabbed Rose's arm, bent it behind his back, and shoved Rose against one of the shuttered blinds—planting his face in it in the process.

Rose snarled, "You don't know who you're dealing with. You just made the biggest mistake of your life."

While still pinning Rose to the window, Walker bent down, picked up the gun, slowly undid the safety so that Rose could hear what he was doing, and whispered in Rose's ear, "You've got it backward, pal. *You* don't know who *you're* dealin' with." Then he held the barrel up to Rose's right temple.

Rose made the mistake of trying to get out of Walker's hold—he attempted to swivel to face Walker, but Walker applied more pressure on his arm and jerked it up, which resulted in a slight cracking sound in Rose's elbow.

Rose cried out from the pain and then spit out, "Shit! I think you broke my arm. You're dead, you know that? My people are going tear you into little shreds."

Walker let out a mocking laugh. "Once again, I think you've got it backward, Harley. *I'm* the one holdin' the gun to *your* head. And I'm the one who took out two of Little Mike's soldiers. I'm sure you know who he is; probably one of your clients. And you are a total piece of crap and a slimy thief. Your only hope of gettin' out of this alive today is to sit at that beautiful desk of yours and write out a confession that you stole the money."

"And why would I do that?"

Walker answered, "Because if you don't, you're dead. Right here, right now. It's as simple as that."

Rose shook his head. "I don't believe you."

Walker pushed him harder into the window. "You want me to shoot out your kneecaps instead, so you'll never walk again? Would that prove to you what I'm capable of?"

Rose went silent for a moment. "No. No. But I'll be as good as dead if I write that confession and my clients find out what I did."

"Well," Walker responded, "I'm goin' to solve that problem for you. You write it out, and I'll keep it. No one is ever goin' to see it after you tell your associates to lay off Peters and his wife and make sure they never get harassed again. But, if I ever hear you've caused them any problem, I'll personally deliver it to your clients and to the media."

"How do I know you won't do that anyway?"

"You don't," Walker replied. "But as I see it, you haven't got much of a bargainin' position here, do you? You're in what they call a total lose-lose situation. Either you write it out and trust me to do what I say, or I kill you. And one more thin', I want you to transfer a half million into Peters's bank account. As compensation for what you've put him and his wife through. I'm sure you can easily find the money, given that you've got that three mil."

Rose craned his neck toward Walker. "I'm telling you, Peters took the money, not me. You've got it all wrong."

Walker shoved Rose's head back against the blinds and poked the gun into his temple even more forcefully. "And I'm telling you that's a SLOG. You wouldn't have gone for your gun if you were innocent, would you have? Now, be a good boy and write out that confession so we can all get on with our lives."

Rose's body went slack. "All right. All right. I'm not going to lose my knees or die over Dave Peters and some money I can easily replace.

"Wait a minute, if I just replace the money, my clients will never know it was ever gone. What about that, Marshal? Doesn't that screw up your little plan?"

Walker grunted and pressed the gun into Rose's head with more pressure. "That wouldn't protect Dave Peters, who knows the truth about what you did, so, no, that's not any kind of a solution that works for me. Now, get to writin' out that confession, or be prepared to lose either your mobility or your life."

Walker spun Rose around and shoved him down into his desk chair. Rose took a sheet of letterhead and a pen off the top of the desk and wrote the confession. Once he was finished, he handed it to Walker. "Will that do?"

Walker, who was standing behind Rose with the gun to the back of his head, had read it while it was being written. "Yep. This'll do just fine."

Rose looked up. "You realize that'll never be admissible in a court of law—you being a marshal or not."

Walker laughed. "It's never goin' to make a court of law, is it? It's either goin' to be in my possession forever—if you do right by the Peterses—or it'll go to the media and your clients."

Rose smirked. "When my clients get done with you, forever isn't going to be very long from now."

"Wrong," Walker countered. "Very wrong, Harley. If you tell your clients to come after me—a US Marshal—they'll want to know why, and you can't tell them. And as for your private goons, trust me when I tell you they'll be dead before they even see me."

"What kind of a marshal are you, Harding? That's not the way marshals act. I've met a few before."

Walker's face lit up into a wide grin. "I'm my own kind of marshal, Rose. I don't give a damn how others do their jobs; I do mine my way. Now, I'm going to take this confession and your little peashooter here with me, and you're goin' to stay in your office for the next five minutes with those blinds closed. Feel free to call anyone you want, but if I see the slats open, or anyone followin' me or botherin' the Peterses, the newspapers and your clients will have some very interestin' reading material. And one last thin', if the half mil isn't in Peters's bank by this time tomorrow, I'll be back. And your elbow won't be the only thing hurtin' you."

Rose snorted. "You're a son of a bitch, Harding."

Walker started to leave the office. "I am, aren't I? Proud of it too. Then again, takes one to know one, doesn't it? Aloha."

Walker closed the door behind him, waved to the girl at the reception desk, who nodded back, and then went out to his car and drove away.

On the drive back to Hana, he called Amanda Peters. She answered on the second ring. "Amanda?"

"Yes."

"This is your White Knight. I just want you to know that everythin' is taken care of, and it's safe for your husband to come home."

"Already?" she asked with breathless incredulity.

"Yep. In fact, by this time tomorrow, a half a million dollars will show up in your bank account as Harley Rose's way of showin' how sorry he is for the trouble he's caused you and Dave."

There was silence on the line until Walker asked, "Are you still there?"

Amanda answered, "Yes. I just can't believe any of this."

Walker grinned. "Believe it. When we find Dave, just make sure he never goes back to that office or uses Rose as a reference."

"How are we going to find Dave? What if he's dead?"

Walker considered the questions, and then said, "He could be dead, but I doubt it. If he was, Rose probably wouldn't have acted the way he did with me. So I'm assumin' your husband's alive and well and hidin' out somewhere. As to how we're goin' to find him, I have an idea in mind, but it'll only work if you call him by a term of endearment, or if he calls you one."

Without any hesitation, Amanda responded, "He calls me 'my beautiful 'i'iwi.' It's a very pretty, colorful red bird. Dave always told me my hair reminded him of it."

Walker turned onto the Hana Highway. "That's excellent. Now here's what we're goin' to do. I want you to make a short video on your cell. Have two or three of your closest friends standin' next to you so when Dave sees it, he'll know you weren't bein' coerced. All you have to say is somethin' like, 'Dave, this is your beautiful 'i'iwi.' It's safe to come home. I miss you. Please call me wherever you are.' Once you do that, I'll get it to all the newspapers, TV and radio stations, and they'll run it. I'll put it online too."

"But what if he's not in Hawaii?"

Walker answered with two questions. "When he left for the run did Dave take much money with him? Has he used a charge card since he disappeared?"

Amanda responded, "Whatever he could put in his shorts pocket, and I checked our charge cards online yesterday, and he hasn't used them. That's why I'm not sure Dave's still alive."

Walker tried to reassure her. "What you just told me makes me pretty sure he hasn't left the islands. He'd need money to do that. As to his being alive, I'm bettin' on it. If he was dead, Rose wouldn't have given a crapola, but he did. So, make that video, and let's get him back to you."

Walker could hear Amanda starting to sob. "Okay. I'll do it. But what if he doesn't come back?"

"Then I'll bring in a tracker I've used before. He can find anyone, anywhere. After you've made that video, post it to my website. I'll take it from there, and you'll have Dave back faster than you can say Speedy Gonzalez."

"Who?"

Walker chuckled. "Never mind. Just a cartoon character I love who's really quick."

After they hung up, and he reached Paia, passing a bar, Walker realized he was looking forward to having a glass of wine and watching the ocean from the rear deck of his house. But he quickly reduced his speed when he saw the Construction Ahead sign and the cars in front of him slowed to a crawl.

CHAPTER SIX

Three mornings later, Walker was sipping a freshly made piping-hot cup of coffee on his back deck, watching two brown boobies do a series of skim-plunge dives into the ocean. He craned his neck when he heard a sound behind his lounge chair. "That you, Sarah?"

"It is," she confirmed, before sitting on the chaise next to him. Holding a partially eaten piece of toast in one hand and a half-filled glass of orange juice in the other, she asked, "Did you see the front page of today's *Maui News*?"

Walker shook his head. "Haven't gotten to it yet. Why?"

Sarah took a bite of her toast before answering. "I just looked at it on my iPhone. It said that this guy who disappeared after running away turned himself in and went back to his wife. I know you were trying to help out and find him. Was that your doing?"

Walker took another sip of his coffee, gave a small nod, and smiled.

Sarah mocked a frown. "So, you're not going to say anything about it? You're not going to tell me how you did it? You're just going to sit there and say zero?"

Walker took another sip, turned to face her, and broke out in a toothy smile. "Yep. No details to share. The White Knight has helped his first maiden in distress, and he doesn't share any of the gory details with anyone."

"Not even me?"

"Especially not you," Walker replied. "Sometimes I'm goin' to have to do some serious stuff to get people the help they need, and you don't need to be burdened with any of that."

Sarah squinted her eyes. "You didn't kill anyone, did you?"

When Walker responded, "Nope," Sarah giggled. "Just checking." Then she added more seriously, "I'm proud of you, Walker. You did a good thing."

He patted her arm. "Thanks, kid. All in a day's work. Glad I could help them out."

DON
BRUNS

LET ME PUT MY LOVE INTO YOU

When you were to kill someone, it took preparation. He wasn't some street thug, some kid who would stand out in a police lineup. No. He'd dressed down. To blend in. Rule number five: *Become one with the surroundings.* You walked down a New York street, the high-end dressers stood out. Fancy ladies with fashionably tight skirts and heels, you took notice. Men in tailored suits and Gucci lace-ups, walking Canal Street in Lower Manhattan, they were recognized.

Ginger Gallagher was dressed in worn jeans, an AC/DC T-shirt with a title from *Back in Black*, "Let Me Put My Love into You," on the back, and knockoff Air Jordan Nikes. His blue Yankees ball cap was pulled low over his forehead. He melded. There were hundreds of pedestrians . . . jeans, sneakers, and logo Ts. Nobody was going to pay attention. When you were going to murder someone, *that* was important.

Tito Taratino was the target. A second-generation Italian, he roamed lower Manhattan, running a string of counterfeit street vendors who openly sold fake Rolex watches, Gucci bags, Dior, Louis Vuitton, Ray-Ban sunglasses, even Apple AirPods. There was over ten million dollars' worth of fake merchandise confiscated by law enforcement in the past year. Probably twenty times more than that was actually sold by unscrupulous street hawkers.

Setting up minimal displays on top of a large blanket or rug, they sold their goods for pennies on the dollar, offering remarkably realistic counterfeit merchandise. A Christian Dior tote that sold for $3,800 would go for $80. The vendor made half. China child labor at its best. Buyers knew they were fake but were taken in with their air of authenticity.

The minute, the second a police car pulled up with a blast of a siren, the moment that a uniformed cop walked into their space, the vendors pulled up the underlying fabric . . . the blanket, the rug, maybe a bed sheet, and covered their merchandise, dragging it to a new location.

Gallagher had followed rule number nine. *Do your homework.* He didn't care why the scumbag on his list needed to die, but he had to understand what motivated the character. Where he or she was (yes, he'd been contracted to kill a couple of women), and places they might frequent.

Gallagher had done his last hit two weeks ago. A banker in Fargo, North Dakota. There were no stipulations, so he'd pulled his hat down low, put on sunglasses and a medical mask, walked into the Second Frontier Bank, asked to speak to the manager, and shot the man in his pinstripe suit through the head as he exited his cubicle, brown bloody brains spattering against the wall behind him. The integrated suppressor keeping the bang to a minimum, Gallagher walked out, dropping the B&T Station Six pistol on the floor. He hated to leave it behind—an expensive piece of equipment, over two thousand dollars—but with vinyl gloves there were no fingerprints, no trace of ownership, and he was paid thirty thousand dollars for the job. Let it go. Someone obviously had felt the man needed to be eliminated.

In the last week, he'd purchased a burner phone from Walmart, established a number, and called the eleven digits for Paladin. Paladin, the person who'd contacted him after his stint in the army as a sniper. Paladin had, in brief terms, told him he could offer a minimum of five hundred thousand dollars a year for minimal service. A very attractive offer considering at that moment he was selling toilets at a hardware store in Wisconsin.

"Please leave a message at the tone."

Nothing else.

"Paladin, this is Tracker. I'm ready for an assignment."

Two days later, Tracker received a call.

"Tracker, your next mission is Tito Taratino. New York City. Manhattan area. He runs a chain of street-side boutiques offering counterfeit luxury items." There was a pause, as if Paladin were assessing the assassination. "We need the elimination in one week. One week, Tracker. By the fifteenth. Forty thousand dollars minus my fifteen percent. Yes or no?" The connection went dead.

He thought about it. For five years now he'd accepted, rejected calls from Paladin . . . *Have Gun Will Travel*. He'd made millions of dollars. Occasionally, he had regrets. Fewer as the years went by. Someone wanted this guy dead. At a very hefty price tag. Rule number ten. *Don't ask why*.

He'd come up with the list of rules on his own. And he sometimes contradicted himself. *Don't ask why*? And he was supposed to kill this person? For no reason he could think of? But he tried to follow the rules. *Don't ask why*. He returned the call.

"Paladin, I'll be in New York in two days. Taking care of business. Mission accepted."

———

The Jitter Bean on Twentieth Street was Tito Taratino's daytime hangout. His evening club was Primo Uno. Five thousand a month just for the dues, but you got to hang with New York's premier players. Comedians from *Saturday Night Live*, his honor the mayor himself. Players from the Giants, the Knicks, and some heavy hitters from the underworld. It amused him to think that some of the rich and famous who were members of Primo Uno were probably wearing some of his counterfeit jewelry, carrying his bags, wearing his Rolex watches.

But during the day, it was the Bean, and today the Bean was very busy, tables crowded with conversationalists, a wide assortment of young people on their computers and their phones. Couples in deep discussions, and business deals happening right in front of him. Taratino breathed in the nutty odor of freshly ground beans, scanning the establishment, the bustling atmosphere. Needing a free space, some independence, he approached a young Asian couple who were engaged in a spirited conversation. Placing his Lenovo ThinkPad on their table, he said, "Get the fuck out. Now. This is my table."

"Excuse me?" The man stood up and stood toe-to-toe with Taratino, staring up at the man's towering ten-inch advantage.

"Excuse *you*? No, I don't think so."

Tito reached down, grabbed the man by the throat, and squeezed. Hard.

"No!" the girl screamed. "Let him go. We will leave."

He hung on a moment longer before the man collapsed on the floor.

She helped him to his feet, grabbed her purse, and they stumbled toward the exit.

Tito sat down, opened the laptop, and his gaze swept the room. Everyone in the packed shop avoided any eye contact. When Tito Taratino walked into an establishment, you left well enough alone.

He didn't approach the counter. The baristas had seen the slim, swarthy-skinned man with combed-back black hair the minute he'd entered the café. The young girl in the yellow-and-red striped apron brought him the red-eye immediately. One shot of espresso and six ounces of drip-brewed coffee. Kept him alert. Kept his senses alive. He nodded when she placed it in front of him.

He studied the screen, scrolling down for messages. There were two that made him cringe.

Tito,

We've made an offer. You have refused us. We countered and you are obviously ignoring our interest. I will ask again for a meeting where we can talk about taking over your business. If I don't hear from you in the next twenty-four hours, we will be forced to take extreme measures. We made a reasonable offer, enough that you can comfortably walk away. Take the offer, Tito. Make it easy on everyone.

FB

Franky Billoti. The Chicago prick. Linked to a street crew in Lincoln Park, he'd branched out into New York where he ran a commercial laundry company and restaurant supply business in Queens. Wasn't that enough? Looking to expand his holdings, he now wanted to control the counterfeit luxury business. A business that Tito had worked hard to organize, busted his ass to set up major connections with Chinese labor camps, hired artists to manufacture items that looked as close to the originals as possible.

The second message made him even madder. Unsigned, he still knew who the son of a bitch was. A guy he'd made very rich with payoffs to keep the cops out of his hair in Manhattan. Lieutenant Bob Stone. A New York prick.

Tito,

Chicago is putting a lot of pressure on us to put a stop to your part of the operation. And they're throwing a lot of incentives our way for us to cooperate. Advice from above. Take the buyout. It saves us all from potential problems.

What was the worst that could happen? Well, *that* would be the worst. Of course. But they couldn't just eliminate him. They'd need a transition. They'd need him to show them the ropes, the suppliers, the logistics . . . This wasn't just some pop-up business that you could take over with the snap of your fingers.

He sipped the red-eye, a bitter jolt to his system.

Unless they had his number two on their side . . .

No. Not possible. She was as faithful as a guard dog. Sandra Gravano. She worked hard, made a lot of money from the enterprise, and worshipped him. Didn't she? Not Sandy, the cute, petite, redheaded associate that he depended on. She helped hire and run the vendors, found new supply chains, and could be tough when she had to be. He'd seen her take down a man twice her size, kneeing him in the groin and making him cry. She could be scary. He'd groomed her to take over the business. Someday. She would have to wait because someday was a long way off.

And there was Annette, his bookkeeper. Annette Barnes actually knew more about the business than anyone. She knew where the money came from; she knew where the payables went. And his business was pretty much all about that. Income stream, payables. You didn't have to be a brain surgeon.

He'd felt vulnerable before but not like this.

The door to the café opened, and a middle-aged punk walked in wearing an AC/DC T-shirt professing "Let Me Put My Love into You," his baggy jeans riding on his bony hips and a Yankee ball cap pulled low over his forehead. The man scanned the room, at one point looking directly at Tito, then walked to the counter and took the only empty seat. The line from Buffalo Springfield's "For What It's Worth" came to him: "Paranoia strikes deep. Into your life it will creep."

Taratino closed the computer, took another sip of the coffee, and shuddered. For five years he'd built this business. He'd run off the competition, shot a competitor through his heart, lied, cheated, threatened and cajoled people. Bought himself a police lieutenant. Big Bob Stone. Things were going very well, then Chicago made a move. Billoti had moved in and within a three-week period, it appeared his growing business, his mini-empire, would collapse if he didn't agree to sell.

Wasn't going to happen.

He picked up his cell phone and texted Sandy. He wanted a meeting, Central Park, in the open. West 89th by the pond. And he'd watch from a distance to see if she really showed up. Alone. In the next hour. She couldn't have sided with the enemy. Couldn't. Still, cops were confiscating more and more merchandise. They knew where to be. Chicago was apparently paying off Stone. Something was going on. Maybe they'd threatened her, maybe it was even more lucrative on the other side. Maybe. Had she turned on him? Chicago seemed to have an abundance of cash and influence. Goddamn Billoti. Everything was going to shit and there was no time to prepare.

Tito pushed back his chair, put a ten-dollar bill on the table, and walked out, his laptop tucked under his arm. Stepping around the overflowing trash can, the McDonald's wrappers and Starbucks cups, rotting banana peels and half-eaten sandwiches, he looked both ways twice before he crossed the street, not certain if there was someone taking aim, ready to erase his legacy as a player in the annals of New York City crime. Nobody but a street bum walking in circles, mumbling to himself.

———

Ginger Gallagher took a quick swallow of his black coffee. Nothing fancy, just coffee. The barista wasn't happy, hoping to make something special and increase his tip. Gallagher subscribed to rule number eight. *Never pay with a card, and never leave a tip that's too little or too much.* He put three bucks on the counter and three quarters. Nothing the barista would remember as being too much or too little.

As he walked out of the door, he caught a glimpse of Tito Taratino turning the corner. He'd found one of his haunts. But rule number seven was *Don't become a regular*, so it wasn't a good idea to go back. Someone might recognize you and remember you had been there. He had three days left. Taratino wasn't hard to track. He had an apartment on East 13th Street and worked from an office in the Sheepshead Bay area of Brooklyn, visiting the office almost every morning. He was easy to track from that point. His office staff consisted of an older woman who apparently worked the books and a young woman named Sandra.

His mission was to eliminate the man. The directions as to how to accomplish that were not so simple. Preferably, make it appear that the man had an accident. Not always easy to do. As a sniper in the army, there were no accidents. He aimed and fired, taking out 97 percent of his targets. Blow their brains out or a heart shot. Not once was there an accident. These jobs, the accidental-death jobs, were always more difficult. They took a lot more thought, a lot more planning.

Push the victim into traffic. Poison them. Shove them down the stairs. Hold their head underwater in a pool. Oh, there were fifty ways to leave your lover. Fifty ways to make it seem there was an accident. But it took more planning. More investigation. More *number nine*. There were eleven rules, but number nine was *Do your homework*. And he believed in that rule. *Do your homework.* He got to know the suspect. His haunts, his schedule, where he hung out, where he ate breakfast, lunch, and dinner.

Tito was a creature of habit. He always had breakfast at the Fat Cat Café on 23rd Street in Long Island City. Pancakes with a fried egg. The suspect wandered, visiting different vendor locations from nine to noon. At twelve he stopped at Fuego's or Johnny D's on Broadway. And two, three times a week, he'd stop at the Bean, midafternoon.

This should be an easy assignment, and he needed to figure out how to put this asshole away. Maybe over a pizza at Johnny's. Maybe he chokes to death. Maybe a taxi does a hit-and-run? There was a major problem with taking someone's life with these directions. You had to make people believe it happened by accident. The dumb jerk walked into the street and didn't see the taxi coming at him. The food was so good, how could it contain poison? A gas explosion. A fire, drug overdose . . .

He walked into the dingy lobby of the Selby, a rundown hotel in Hell's Kitchen. Room 206. This wasn't a rifle-sniper attack. This was an ingenious, creative attack. In the next three days, find a way to smoke this scumbag. Find a way to dispose of him, where people would applaud his demise . . . but never believe it was planned.

And number nine, the "do your homework" rule, also had him searching websites regarding counterfeit luxury items. Just for fun he ran up the statistics. Worldwide, the gross was 1.3 trillion dollars a year. Not million, not billion, but *trillion.* And he thought about how he was being paid several thousand dollars to put a guy out of business who was involved in a trillion . . . trillion . . . trillion-dollar scam. It wasn't that his life wasn't good. He made a lot of money, but trillions of dollars? Seriously, trillions. He'd looked it up. One million dollars a day for three thousand years. That equated to over one trillion dollars. Holy mother of God.

He vowed to revisit his profession after this hit. He owed the kill to Paladin, but damn. There was serious money involved here.

———

Tito Taratino stood behind a boathouse, glancing at the clearing on Sailboat Pond where he'd asked Sandy to meet him. He was a little early. His limo driver was waiting in a parking lot a block away. Kids with remote-controlled vessels put their boats through intricate maneuvers, and several full-sized sailboats worked their way across the water.

Sandy was a hustler before he'd hired her. The reason he hired her. She'd tried to hustle him, offering discounted counterfeit tickets to Knicks games. He knew, just by the way she approached him, that she wasn't on the up-and-up. Besides, he was a Brooklyn Nets fan.

"You and your printer might have a good con going, but I think I can up the ante," he'd told her. And she'd listened. He wasn't sure she still didn't push tickets on the side, but she'd been good for his business. She wasn't afraid to use her good looks, her obvious physical attributes including a trim waist, cute butt, and generous boobs. And of course her intellect. She used those to get what she wanted. What *they* wanted. Sandy was a kindred spirit. She would do whatever it took to reach the goal. He appreciated that.

There was a wooded area across the sun-dappled lake, a couple of benches down by the water. He patiently waited, knowing she was a little late to most meetings. And ten minutes later, there she was. By herself. No sign of anyone backing her up. Tito had been pretty sure she wasn't double-crossing him. She wasn't giving Chicago inside information. Would never work against him with Lieutenant Bob Stone.

Sandy, his loyal partner. She sat on a bench, looking to her right and left, and he left his shelter and walked around the lake, waving as he approached her.

"Tito. What's the emergency."

"Not an emergency," he said. "A concern. A question."

"Which is?"

"You know that Franky Billoti is threatening us." He used the word "us." Make her sure she was part of the team.

"Of course, I'm aware. It's all you talk about. Billoti this, Billoti that."

"Just got a note from Bob Stone. He's getting pressure from Billoti."

"That doesn't surprise me. Okay. And what are your plans?"

Tito paused. The shouting of young people from the other side of the lake traveled across the still water. The gentle breeze sounded like a soft whisper as it passed through the trees.

"First of all, I need to know whose side you are on."

The girl stood up and he watched her. Tight jeans, a black T-shirt just short enough to expose her toned midriff. Her fiery red hair spilling down her face and over her shoulders. She was beautiful, sexy, and obviously devoted to him. Her expression was that of anger.

"You're questioning my loyalty? After everything I've given you? How could you do that?"

"I need to know. Give me the truth. It seems someone is trying to sabotage our business."

She shook her head.

"Tito." Her tone was now sad. "Tito, Tito, Tito."

"Yeah, but if they waste me, if I'm out of the picture, you and Annette are the only people who know how the organization works. You see where I'm going with this. They need that information."

"Tito, you saved me. You gave me a chance even after I tried to screw you. I owe you. Come here and hold me. How can you question my feelings?"

Tito stood up, putting his arms around the petite girl. He hugged her, aware of her soft breasts pressing against his chest. He smiled, immediately feeling the sharp, piercing pain in his ribcage, the sudden thrust into his heart. The intense burning sensation that spread through his chest and the slow, relaxing feel of drifting into unconsciousness. It all happened so fast.

The last feeling he was aware of, shocking cold water, startling his senses, then breathing in the liquid, gurgling, choking, strangling, and then it was over.

———

Rule number four almost always came into play. *Be prepared for anything.* That was difficult. But the idea was, be ready at any moment to pivot. Don't panic, don't hesitate. Be ready for everything to turn to shit. And resolve that you will immediately figure out your next move. After all, there was a lot of money at stake. Hell, there was his life at stake.

When his burner phone rang, he focused on rule number four. Paladin never called in the middle of a mission. He paused, then calmly answered.

"Paladin?"

"Abort the current mission."

"Obviously you know it's not completed?"

"What I know is, someone else took care of the problem."

Number four. Number four. Take a deep breath and figure out the next step.

"I had three more days and . . ."

"There was an opportunity and that opportunity was taken."

"Then there's the time, effort, money . . ."

"There's another mission. You will be rewarded."

Gallagher was quiet.

"There's a Chicago gangster, Franky Billoti."

"So I go to Chicago?"

"No. No. He's currently working in New York. He owns a commercial laundry company and a restaurant supply company in Queens. Gold Medal Laundry. Supply Depot Restaurant Company."

"This is a first."

"Not for me. It's happened before." Paladin let go a breath. "He's involved in your current mission. Taking over Tito's business. Just a point of reference. He needs to go."

"Time frame?"

"Our client would like it to happen sooner than later."

"Of course."

"Just do the job and disappear. He's a made man. There will be no surprise that someone wanted the job done. Okay?"

"Any way I want?"

"Disposal is up to you."

"And compensation is . . ."

"For your time and effort already performed, half the agreed amount."

Twenty thousand and he didn't have to kill Tito.

"For your new assignment, another forty. Just get it done."

"I accept."

"Tracker . . ." Paladin paused.

"Yes?"

"This Billoti, as I said, he wants to take over Tito's business. Be careful. There's a female who . . ."

Silence.

"Who what?"

"She is our client. I've probably said too much. Just be careful."

He was. Careful. Always. And now, a bit confused. But there were multiple factors. Someone had killed Tito. Still, there was money on the table for the work he'd done. Then there was a new target. Some made guy named Franky. And Paladin had made a veiled threat regarding a female.

Rule number six. *Don't overthink the assignment.* With all these components, it was damned hard not to. Damned hard.

———

The Gravano name was Italian. There was Salvatore "Sammy the Bull" Gravano, who served in the Gambino crime family. There was William "Billy the Butcher" Gravano who worked for the Massati family, but as far as Sandra Gravano knew, there were no crime families in her background.

It didn't mean she wasn't starting a new legacy. She'd been a thief, a counterfeiter, a thug, and, to make ends meet, sometimes a hooker. She'd distributed narcotics, and now she was a murderer. You could eventually add her name to the list of *famous* Gravano criminals. Sandra "Sandy the Sadist" Gravano. That wasn't her goal. She just wanted what she considered was rightfully hers. She'd worked overtime to make this business prosperous. Whatever it took. And when some mafioso guy came out of nowhere and seemed poised to take over, it was time to step up. She'd drawn up a plan. The first part of the plan was to get rid of the weakest link.

Some ancient philosopher once said, "The end justifies the means." She subscribed to that theory. The truth was, if you didn't look out for yourself, you were screwed. Nobody out there was going to look out for you. Tito, a weak link, would have turned on her in a second if she meant his future was in jeopardy. And, of course, it was. He just hadn't figured it out. It was nothing personal. Strictly a business decision.

And now there were two more to deal with. Franky Billoti and Lieutenant Bob Stone. The hired gun she'd employed from Paladin would hopefully deal with Billoti. She'd paid enough for that to happen. So, Big Bob was the stumbling block. The corpulent cop liked his weekly check and would go to work for the highest bidder, but Sandy had another cop in mind. Someone who might trade sexual favors for less money, and she just didn't trust Stone. She'd already made the sexual move on the younger, more attractive officer, Davin Treat, so she was pretty sure he would fit in nicely. He did so in other ways as well.

Get rid of the Chicago mob guy. Blow Stone's cover so the NYPD would have to investigate and end up firing him.

Gravano walked into the office the next morning and found Annette already at her desk.

"Annette, I'm sure you heard?"

"I did," the lady said quietly. She pointed to the newspaper in front of her. "The *Post* only printed it on the *front page*. Hard to ignore." The ghoulish headline read GANGSTER GORE WASHES UP ON SHORE.

"It's terrible."

"For him. But for you . . . you're next in line." The lady gave her a faint smile. "Funny how that worked out."

"Well," Sandy paused, brushing her luscious mane of red hair back, "I suppose that . . ."

"I make all the deposits, I sign all of the checks," Annette said. "Except mine. If we still have a business here, and I assume we do, who signs my paycheck? I need to know. And I think it's time for a raise. We can discuss how much."

Gravano studied the woman. Annette Barnes. Midfifties; short, cropped hair; severe frown lines etched into her forehead. High-collar blouse and skirt far below her knees. Someone who was not to be messed with. Like the Bond movie villainess in *From Russia with Love*. Rosa Klebb. The lady who had blades in her shoes and tried to kill Sean Connery. Watch out.

"*I* do," she said. "I sign your paycheck. From now on." Singular. *I.* "Okay?"

"Just wanted to know."

So much for sympathy. So much for compassion. Barnes controlled the finances. Cold, hard, steady, she ran the money side of things. An important entity. Sandy decided she could work with this woman. One less complication.

———

Billoti was a mess. Petty theft, physical assaults, and grand larceny. He was in and out of jail in his teens; two years in prison in his twenties; charges of sex trafficking, armed robbery, racketeering, smuggling, and running drugs in his thirties. Chicago, being rather lax on sentencing, bailouts, and crime in general, gave Franky a pass on most of his transgressions. He looked at his odds and, figuring New York wasn't far behind Chicago on leniency, he added that city to his quests in his forties. You could get away with a lot in the Big Apple.

A laundry that catered to major hotels, a restaurant supply company that supplied most of the high-end eateries with everything from silverware to china, coffee makers to wine decanters. Billoti was making some good scratch. All with a little Mafia threat. A little push from organized crime. It was the way he made money in the Windy City, and why not here? Then he heard about Tito Taratino and his scam on counterfeit luxury items. Fake jewelry from Tiffany, Patek Philippe watches, Gucci bags . . . looking good. He'd had staff purchase some of the items, and they were close to the originals, at a fraction of the price of the originals. And Tito Taratino, a small-time hustler, was ripe for a takeover.

Franky Billoti was in a perfect position to buy out that multimillion-dollar operation. Maybe it was time to put the counterfeiter on the sidelines. He had a plan. Offer him a little money. If that didn't work, intimidation. Threaten the tin-pan Italian with an Italian-based gang from Chicago. A true mafioso front. Scare the bejesus out of him.

So far, that wasn't working. Then Billoti woke up to see the cover of the *New York Post*. A graphic black-and-white photo. Tito had been murdered and washed up on the shores of a lake in Central Park. Holy crap. There was no better time to swoop.

The mobster was aware that the basic operation was run by Taratino and two women. The buying, collections from vendors, interaction with law enforcement . . . all run by three people. Oh, the vendors played a key role and were first in the line of fire if the cops raided their booth. They stood to face up to ten years in prison if convicted. But the organization had been designed by Taratino. And the two women he employed were responsible for its success. One, a Gravano. He'd looked it up. No relation to Sammy the Bull. That could have been difficult. Sammy was out, doing a podcast about his history in crime, but Billoti wanted nothing to do with him. The guy was dangerous as hell. No relation to Billy the Butcher, who was doing fifteen years in the Fishkill Correctional Facility in Beacon, New York.

The other lady, an accountant. Annette Barnes. Just someone who handled the books. Counted the money and balanced it against inventory. Simply a clerk. No big deal. How hard would this be now that Tito was out of the picture?

The Gravano girl had information that he would need, and he could offer her a payroll position until he had learned how the operation worked. He'd rather have learned the business from Taratino, but this would have to do.

Franky Billoti decided to pay the office a visit. Surely the Gravano chick knew the story. Tito had certainly prepped her. And, if he hadn't, it was time she knew the score. While he had a backup team of a dozen soldiers, she had a bookkeeper and vendors. Vendors who he felt certain would roll over the minute he announced there was a new boss in town. They wanted to keep their jobs. He wanted them to continue producing. It was that simple.

He Uber'd a ride to the Sheepshead Bay office in Brooklyn, not really certain that the office would be staffed at this point. The boss was dead, and the Italian chick and the bookkeeper might have taken off. Who knew? But now was the time to take control. Before it became a free-for-all. Make the takeover a seamless transition. There were millions of dollars at stake.

As he exited the Nissan Sentra, as he walked toward the office building, he had no idea what was out there, but he was anxious to find out. That's what he lived for. *Lived for.*

———

He felt the Walther PK380 pressing against his hip. The gun with the laser. It only made sense that the mafia guy would approach the office. Billoti had to make peace or kill the women who were left. So Ginger Gallagher had planted himself half a block from the brick structure. In a courtyard park with leafy tree cover and a semi-comfortable gray metal bench. He sat on that bench, waiting. A sniper, as good or bad as they may be, had one common virtue. Patience. A minute, an hour, a day, a week . . . patience.

But he didn't need to wait long. He'd studied photographs. There was no question; this was Franky Billoti. And the mobster was being dropped off at the entrance of the building. Maybe thirty seconds before he entered, and then he would be lost from sight until he exited, and who knows what kind of damage he could inflict during that time?

Rule number one. *Be quick.*

He pointed the pistol, with laser-sharp accuracy, and pulled the trigger, slow and easy. Billoti stumbled and fell. Heart shot. Textbook. The target was eliminated. One of three homicides that day in the Big Apple. Nothing unusual.

Rule number three. *Use a generic rental car.* He got behind the wheel of the Toyota Corolla, settled in, and punched in the numbers on his burner phone.

"Tracker?"

"Mission accomplished."

"Call if you need work."

He would. Gallagher pushed the Send key, activating the virus he'd installed. The phone screen went blank. Getting out of the car, he placed the plastic device under the rear wheel, got back in, and backed up, crushing the phone. That should take care of the situation. Another successful mission. Another use of the eleven hit man rules.

———

Five minutes later she stepped out of the cab, seeing the body sprawled by the door. A homeless addict? But dressed a little better than . . .

"Oh my god." She whispered. Franky Billoti. Sandra stepped around the corpse and entered the building, taking the elevator to the sixth floor.

The Barnes lady was at her desk, working her computer keyboard.

"Franky Billoti is lying in a pool of blood outside our building." Sandra shook her head.

Annette looked up and gave her a grim smile.

"Kind of fortuitous . . . for you."

"And you are implying?"

"Pretty much locks you in as the new CEO. Now, about my raise."

"Jesus, Annette, there's a dead body outside our . . ."

"There was a dead body in Central Park. There will be dead bodies on a daily basis. Come on. This is New York City."

"We have things to discuss."

"Oh yes, we do." Barnes stood up, staring beyond the redhead to the office behind her.

"Look, Annette, I'm sure we can arrive at an equitable figure. You are important to the organization and . . ."

She felt hands on her throat, squeezing tightly. Shaking her head, raising her hands, she desperately tried to dislodge the strong grasping fingers. The woman kicked back, striking her attacker's shins but accomplishing nothing. She saw flashes of light, black and white. She attempted a gasp, but there was no air left to breathe, and her head seemed to explode. The lady collapsed as her attacker lowered her to the floor.

"Never actually killed someone before," he said. "Kind of a power rush."

"We're going to make this thing happen," Annette said. "You work your side, I'll work mine. We can make a ton of money here, Bob."

Bob Stone nodded.

"I'll take her down the back elevator, put her in the dumpster two blocks down. I don't believe anyone will ever find the body."

Annette Barnes smiled. She also believed the end justified the means. And the means meant millions of dollars. She went back to her computer and plugged in figures. Business as usual.

ANDREW CHILD

YOU SHOOK ME ALL NIGHT LONG

Major William Hunt sat on the bench at the east side of the central square in the sleepy little town of Massenstadt, West Germany. That was what he had been directed to do. His instructions had been clear. Dress as normal. Carry a briefcase. Bring no other luggage. Nothing that would tip anyone watching that when he left his home that morning, it would be for the last time. He had been in the US Army for fifteen years. The first four he had spent at West Point. The other eleven in Germany, with his latest post at the headquarters of the 66th Military Intelligence Brigade at the Wiesbaden Army Airfield. And that afternoon he was set to become the second officer in a fortnight to defect from his unit.

The first officer to defect from Six-Six-MI had been a captain. His name was Adam O'Neill. He had been smuggled out of Germany on a cargo ship, transferred to a submarine, then a plane, and finally ferried by helicopter to an officially obsolete Red Army base near Yekaterinburg, deep inside the USSR. He had also been carrying only a briefcase. Its contents would have been worth tens of millions of dollars on the open market, but O'Neill wasn't interested in the money. He was a rarity in the world of espionage—a true believer. The only reward he craved was to be recognized as a Hero of the Soviet Union. Which was going to happen, he had been assured, the moment he completed his deprogramming—a two-week-long process that was necessary to cleanse him of any taint of capitalism that lingered from his years of exposure to the decadent west.

Hunt waited in the square, alone, for five minutes. Then another person approached him. A woman. She looked like she was a couple of years younger than him. She was slim and blond and athletic. Her hair was backcombed and lacquered, and her blue dress had ruffles on the skirt and wide, puffy shoulders. She eased down onto the bench next to him, slid nearer, and wrapped her arm around his shoulder. She leaned in close like she was going to kiss his cheek, but instead she whispered in his ear.

"Do you have it?" she said.

Hunt nodded. He patted the briefcase.

The woman stood up. "Good. Come on. Time to go."

Hunt said, "How will we get there?"

"We'll walk."

"I mean, how will we get to Moscow?"

The woman shook her head. "We're not going to Moscow. Not yet. First, we need to see what you brought us. Verify it. If it's what you promised, then we'll go."

Deep lines creased Hunt's forehead. "So where are you taking me now?"

"Not far. Somewhere safe. You have nothing to worry about. Unless you lied to us."

Hunt's face relaxed. "I didn't lie. The material is genuine. I give you my word. Run any test you want. You'll see."

Major Hunt had nothing to worry about, but Joe Reacher did. He was sitting in his office in the Pentagon, four thousand and fifty miles away, and he knew exactly what Hunt was doing. He knew exactly what was in Hunt's briefcase. He knew it was genuine. He knew the damage it could cause in the Soviets' hands. And he was responsible for the plan to make sure that no harm would be done—by Hunt's secrets, or by

O'Neill's. The plan was high risk. Extremely high. It sat smack in the middle of *deniable* territory. The kind of operation that no one would ever know about if it worked but would see him hung out to dry if it failed. It would be denounced as an unauthorized blunder dreamed up by a deranged maverick. Not how he wanted his career to end. That was for damn sure. So he was trying not to think about all the things that could go wrong. And all the things he didn't know. Starting with where the KGB agent would take Hunt so that her comrades could begin the process of authenticating the documents he was carrying. He knew they had a safe house in Mainz and another in Frankfurt. Mainz is closer to Massenstadt, which would mean less travel time, so less exposure. Frankfurt is larger, which would mean it was easier to hide. Joe had both places covered. But the KGB also had safe houses in Munich and Cologne and Hannover. If they chose one of those, things were going to get difficult, fast. And if they had a base someplace else—someplace new—things would get worse still.

The same time Hunt was leaving the square in Massenstadt with the KGB agent, Jack Reacher, Joe's younger brother, was walking into the bar at the Estrel Hotel in Mainz. He was wearing tight stonewashed jeans, black motorcycle boots, a black T-shirt, and a leather jacket with a denim vest stretched over it. He was carrying a beaten-up leather duffel in one hand and a giant radio / cassette player in the other. It was more than three feet wide. Its front was covered with knobs and dials and lights and sliders, and it had an enormous detachable speaker at each end. Everything about it was designed to give the impression of ear-bursting loudness, even when it was switched off.

There were twelve other customers in the Estrel's bar. Four couples at separate small tables spread around the edge of the room and a group of four friends at a larger table in the center. Some of them were older than Reacher. Some were younger. But all of them were far more smartly dressed. They all had glasses in front of them. Some had white wine. Some had genteel cocktails. But no one was sucking down their drinks. It wasn't that kind of a place. Their conversations stalled when

Reacher appeared. He was six feet five. His chest was like a beer barrel. His arms were like telegraph poles. He glanced at each disapproving face in turn and strolled the rest of the way to the bar. He dumped his bag and his stereo on the floor, pulled out a stool, sat down, and beckoned to the bartender.

He said, "*Bitte einen Liter Bier,*" took a ten Deutschmark bill from his pocket, and laid it on the bar.

Back in Massenstadt, the KGB agent threaded her arm through Hunt's and slowed him down a little.

She said, "Take it easy. We're lovers, out for a romantic stroll. Not competitors in a race."

Another couple left their table at an outdoor café at the edge of the square. They were both average height. Average build. They were wearing bland, unremarkable clothes. The kind of people you could stand next to in a bar or sit near at a football match and not be able to describe a minute after you left.

The people Joe Reacher had sent to keep tabs on Hunt.

The agent strolled next to Hunt, chatting about nothing in particular and glancing in the windows of the shops they passed, trying to spot anyone tailing them. She waited for a break in the traffic then led the way across the street. She stopped outside a bookstore. Pretended to look at its display of bestsellers. Waited for a bus to approach from the opposite direction. Started moving again when it was twenty yards away. Tightened her grip on Hunt's arm. And when the bus drew level with them, she dragged him sideways into a shop that rented out costumes for parties and carnivals.

The next person to enter the bar at the Estrel Hotel was a woman. Every eye in the place was on her as she walked across the room. She would be maybe five ten in bare feet but the heels of her black leather boots added three more inches. Her legs were long and toned, and she was wearing the shortest skirt some of the other patrons had ever seen outside the pages of a magazine. She had a stylized version of a biker's jacket, cropped and cinched in to emphasize her waist, which was tiny, and her chest, which was not. Her blouse was black lace, cut low. Her skin was pale. Her hair was long and so dark it was almost purple. She kept going, apparently oblivious to the stares, and took the stool two away from Reacher.

The bartender kept his distance. He said, in German, "Are you a guest of the hotel, miss?"

The woman glanced at Reacher, then replied, "That remains to be seen."

The bus continued on its way. The couple Joe Reacher had sent could no longer see Hunt or the KGB agent. They'd been there one second and were gone the next. It was a neat trick—simple, and well executed—but it was one the watchers had been expecting. The woman ducked into the next shop on her side of the street. It sold dresses. She took up a position by a rack near the window which gave a good view of both sidewalks. The man turned around and hurried back to the next intersection. He looped around so that he was on the street behind the costume store and joined a line at a bus stop.

Two minutes later Hunt and the agent stepped out through a plain, unmarked door. They had changed their clothes. The agent had swapped her blue dress for a red one. Hunt had ditched his suit in favor of jeans and a T-shirt, but he was still carrying his briefcase. The agent unlocked a car that was parked at the side of the street. A small silver BMW. She slid in behind the wheel and Hunt climbed into the passenger seat. Then she pulled away, made a right at the end of the block, and disappeared into the passing traffic.

The woman ordered a Malibu and pineapple. The bartender pretended not to understand her American accent and then took his time preparing the drink. She waited for him to finally set it down on a mat in front of her, then said, "Let me ask you a question. Is this a library?"

The bartender looked puzzled. "I don't follow."

"It's so damn quiet in here I figured I must have come to a library by mistake. How about some music?"

"We don't generally have music on Tuesdays."

"Did I ask what you generally have?"

The bartender didn't answer.

The woman said, "Music. Now. Come on."

The bartender said, "I can't."

"Why not?"

"I would have to speak with my supervisor."

"Go speak with him, then."

"I can't."

"Why not?"

"I'm not permitted to leave the bar unattended."

The woman shrugged, then turned to Reacher and gestured toward his stereo. "That thing run on batteries?"

The bartender sighed theatrically and said, "Fine. I'll see what I can do."

Joe Reacher's guy stepped away from the line at the bus stop and took his radio out of his pocket. He called in the KGB agent's license plate and a description of her vehicle, then turned and made his way back to the dress shop to collect his partner. Their work was done for the day. The next stage would be down to their colleagues in the cars. There were four of them, all set up to look like taxis. One was circling to the east. One to the west. One to the north. One to the south. Between them they would pick up Hunt and the agent. They would take turns following them. They were expecting at least one more change of vehicle. Probably another spell on foot. Maybe another change of clothes. They knew the KGB's methods well. They just had no way to anticipate which safe house they were going to use.

The woman drained her glass in one gulp, then went to use the bathroom. Twelve pairs of eyes followed her as she left the bar. Their stares weren't friendly. And they weren't welcoming when she came back in. She took her time to cross the room. She smiled at the men. She blanked the other women. And when she climbed onto her stool and crossed her legs, she made sure she was showing plenty of thigh.

Reacher finished the last mouthful of his beer and beckoned to the bartender. "Another beer, *bitte*. And the same again for the lady."

The bartender sneered at the word *lady* but did as he was asked. Slowly, and with a marked lack of enthusiasm.

The woman climbed down and nodded toward the stool next to Reacher. "Do you mind?"

Reacher said, "Be my guest."

The woman settled herself facing Reacher, side toward the room. She crossed her legs even higher. "I'm Nikki."

"Reacher."

"Good to meet you."

"Likewise."

"I've got to ask you something. What's a guy like you doing here?"

"A guy like me?"

"Look at these other stiffs. Are you like them? I bet none of them's had a minute's fun in their lives. And that's before I get to the sticks up their asses. Look at that guy." Nikki nodded toward the man at the nearest table. "It's so far up there I bet he can see it when he cleans his teeth."

The guy shuffled in his seat. The woman who was with him shot daggers in return.

Reacher shrugged. "I heard there might be something going on around here, tonight."

Nikki said, "Looks like you were misinformed. Although, that could change. If your luck holds up."

The KGB agent's BMW was picked up by one of Joe Reacher's fake taxis. The one covering the east of Massenstadt. It followed the BMW along the main road out of town for a couple of miles, sometimes three cars behind, sometimes four, until they arrived at the turnoff for a giant supermarket. The agent pulled into the parking lot and dumped the BMW in a handicapped space near the entrance to the building. She jumped out. Hunt followed a moment later, and she took him by the hand and led the way into the store.

Joe's guy picked up his radio and called for the taxi that was north of the town to come and relieve him. He sent the taxi from the south to monitor the route east, toward Frankfurt. He left the taxi to the west where it was. And he pulled his own car behind a giant RV, out of sight but ready to provide backup if needed.

Hunt and the KGB agent reappeared after ten minutes. The agent had swapped her red dress for white jeans, sneakers, and a tie-dye T-shirt. Hunt had switched to black pleated pants and a baggy houndstooth sweater. He was still clutching his briefcase. She threaded her arm through his and steered him to the center of a row in the middle of the parking lot. To a dark-blue hatchback. A Volkswagen. A car so ubiquitous in Germany as to be practically invisible. Hunt climbed into the passenger seat. The agent got in behind the wheel. Pulled forward out of the space. Followed the signs to the exit. And turned to the southwest. Toward Mainz.

Reacher had swiveled around on his barstool so that he was facing Nikki. She had leaned in a little closer. He had done the same. Her voice had grown louder. He had laughed at some of the things she had said. She had touched his shoulder. His arm. His thigh. But any further progress was interrupted by a guy in a suit. It looked expensive but conservative. He was the kind of man who tried to take care of his appearance. That was clear. But he was losing the battle. The years were overtaking him. He was maybe in his midfifties. His face was flushed. His waist was thickening. His hair was thinning. And the skin on his neck above his collar was puckered like a chicken's.

"Excuse me, sir." The guy crowded in close to Reacher. He kept his voice barely above a whisper. "I'm afraid I'm going to have to ask you to finish your drink and leave. You too, miss."

Reacher picked up his glass, examined the contents, then set it back down. He said, "Have to?"

"What do you mean?"

"You *have to* ask us? Why? Have we broken some kind of law?"

"No, but—"

"Is someone holding your family hostage? Are your kids going to die if we stay here?"

"Of course not. But—"

"Because here's the problem. We've done nothing wrong. And we're not ready to leave. If you want us to go, you'll have to make it worth our while."

"I'm the manager here. I have to consider my other customers. My regulars. And you're making them uncomfortable. You're uncouth. There have been complaints. So I'm asking you nicely. Please leave."

"And if we don't?"

"I'll have no option. I'll have to call the police."

"How long will they take to come?"

"Not long."

"But they're not here already. And they don't have magic powers. The laws of physics still apply. So they won't appear immediately. It'll take them some time. Five minutes? Ten?"

"Perhaps."

"So ask yourself this. If we're making people uncomfortable by sitting and talking, what do you think we could do in ten minutes? Maybe longer if there are some actual crimes taking place to occupy the police tonight."

The manager didn't answer.

Reacher said, "OK. We didn't come here looking for trouble. Maybe we should try to find a compromise. We could go somewhere more private. Carry on there."

"That's an excellent idea."

"Somewhere more private, like a room. Here, in the hotel."

"That wasn't quite—"

"Nikki, do you like to dance? We could push some tables aside. Make some space. Hopefully none of the furniture would get broken . . ."

The manager held both hands up, chest height, palms out. "A room will be fine. Come with me. I'll have someone arrange it."

Reacher shook his head. "You arrange it. We'll stay here. You can bring us the key."

The manager sighed, then turned to go. He said, "Fine. Just behave until I get back. Please."

"One more thing. We want room twelve."

The manager turned back. "Room twelve? No. I'm sorry. That's not possible."

"Why? I know it's not taken. I looked at your register on my way in."

"That room is not in service at present. It has maintenance issues."

"What kind of issues?"

"General upkeep."

"Is there a gas leak?"

"Of course not."

"Toxic mold?"

"No."

"Bed bugs?"

"No!"

"Does it have a bed?"

"Obviously."

"Then we'll take it."

"You won't. I told you. It's not available."

"Then make it available."

"I don't have the authority."

"You said you're the manager. Make an executive decision."

"I don't know. I need to make a call." The guy turned and started for the exit. "Just don't upset anyone else until I get back," he said over his shoulder.

The KGB agent was well-trained at resisting a tail. That was clear. On the highway she varied her speed dramatically, one minute racing ahead and putting empty space between her and any cars that could be used for cover, the next slowing right down so that the vehicles behind her were forced to overtake. She stopped—illegally—at the center of the bridge that crossed the Rhine. And when she reached the city, she timed her passage through the traffic so carefully that more often than not she nipped through intersections right as the lights were turning red. She was so good that within five minutes of leaving the supermarket the driver of the lead taxi decided to gamble. He sped away from the VW and raced ahead to the Mainz safe house.

The safe house was actually an apartment. It was on the second floor of a plain, anonymous building attached to a small hotel. A good location, the guy driving the taxi thought. For the KGB, because the constant ebb and flow of hotel guests would act as cover for anyone arriving or leaving at odd hours, or who was burdened with luggage, or was wearing foreign-looking clothes. And for him, because he could pull up behind a couple of real cabs that were waiting on the far side of a sign that said "Loading and unloading—Hotel Estrel guests only."

The gamble paid off. Joe Reacher's guy didn't see where the KGB agent ditched the VW but he had a clear view as she approached on foot, leading Hunt, who was still clutching his briefcase. Her body looked relaxed, like walking up to the building was no more exciting than returning from a dull day at the office, but her eyes were darting left and right, scanning the street and the sidewalk. She paused at the door, pretending to fumble for her keys, and checked both directions before working the lock and ushering Hunt inside.

The door from the landing to the apartment looked ordinary from the outside, but on the inside it was covered with a bunch of heavy-duty locks and bolts. Two men were waiting in the hallway. They weren't tall, but they were broad and solid with square, shaved heads. They were wearing dark, slightly shiny suits and looked to be in their midtwenties. The sight of them stopped Hunt dead in his tracks.

The agent said, "Don't worry. They're here to keep you safe."

Hunt said, "Safe from what?"

The agent shook her head and guided Hunt into the living room. Next to that was a kitchen, then a bathroom and two bedrooms. The furniture in all the rooms was plain and functional. There was no TV. No pictures on the walls. All the drapes were closed. The air was stale, and it carried a hint of cheap cleaning products.

The agent gave Hunt a moment to take in his surroundings, then said, "Ground rules. Stay away from the windows. Do not open any drapes. Do not answer if anyone knocks on the door. Do not make any noise that the neighbors or the hotel guests could hear. Do not evacuate if you hear a fire alarm or sirens. Understand?"

Hunt nodded. "How long do I have to be here?"

"Depends how quickly your documents check out."

"Good. That shouldn't take long. How do we make it happen?"

"A comrade will arrive shortly. He'll take the papers to Bonn. To an expert. Assuming—"

"No." Hunt clutched the briefcase to his chest.

"Excuse me?"

"No. The documents do not leave my sight."

"I told you. They must be verified. I was clear from the outset. If you won't let them be examined, what kind of message are you sending?"

Hunt heard a sound behind him. It was one of the other men. He had moved into the doorway, almost filling its width.

The agent snapped her fingers to get Hunt's attention. "I really hope you're not playing some kind of game here, Will. Because if you are, it's not going to end well. I promise you."

Hunt shook his head. "No game. I know the documents need to be checked. I want them to be checked. They're real, and they're dynamite. Your people are going to be blown away. But here's the thing. They're all I have. My passport. My meal ticket. My raison d'être. I've walked away from my job. My country. My life. I'm not letting go of them. Your expert can come to me."

The agent was silent for a moment, then she nodded her head. "I understand. But our expert cannot leave the embassy. It's too dangerous. So how about this? The courier will take one page, chosen at random, so that the paper can be tested, and he'll photograph the rest."

Joe Reacher's guy pulled away from the other waiting cabs and dumped his taxi on a side street a couple hundred yards away. He swapped his shoes for a pair of motorcycle boots, pulled on a leather jacket, and hurried back to the entrance of the Hotel Estrel. He went inside, walked through reception, and stopped at the door to the bar.

"Hey!" the guy yelled. "Nikki! The hell are you doing with that bozo?"

The guy strode past the eight remaining guests and leaned in so his head was close to Nikki's. He whispered, "You're green to go." Then he straightened up and said, "What are you waiting for? Come on. We're leaving."

Nikki shook her head. "I'm staying."

The guy grabbed Nikki's arm. "No. You're coming with me."

Nikki tried to pull free. "Let go! I'm not going anywhere with you. It's over between us, you jackass. What do I need to do? Tattoo it on your forehead so you get a reminder whenever you look in the mirror?"

The guy tightened his grip. "I know you don't mean that. Come home. I'll make it up to you. That girl meant nothing to me. It only happened a couple of times. I don't even know her name."

"You think that makes it better? 'Cause it doesn't. It makes me hate you even more. So for the last time. Let. Go."

The guy yanked Nikki's arm.

Nikki yelped.

Reacher said, "Hey, pal. What's your name?"

The guy said, "None of your business."

Reacher kept his voice calm and quiet. "Strange. You must have had a tough time at school. Now here's my real question. The lady asked you to let go of her arm. Why haven't you done that?"

"Stay out of this."

"Here's a thought. Grab my arm instead. See what happens."

The couple at the closest table abandoned their drinks and scuttled to the exit. The other half-dozen guests stayed silent and looked down at the floor.

The guy let go of Nikki. Reacher slid down from his stool. The guy bounced up onto the balls of his feet, but he was still four inches shorter. Reacher took a step forward. Then he caught movement from the doorway. The manager was back.

"Enough." The manager said. "I'm calling the police."

Reacher grabbed the taxi guy by the lapels and lifted him off the ground. He said, "Are you sure that's wise? This guy's heavier than he looks. Could do a lot of damage if I dropped him on a table. Or on the bar. Or on you."

The manager said, "Put him down. Please. There's no need for anyone to get hurt."

"I'll put him down. No one will get hurt. Nothing will get broken. But only when you bring me the key to room twelve."

"How about eleven? Or ten?"

"How's your insurance? Premium all up to date?"

"Why room twelve? What's so special about it? No one's used it for years. It's probably filthy. Eleven's bigger. And ten's nicer, no doubt about it."

Reacher said nothing.

"All right then, fine." The manager ducked through the doorway and returned thirty seconds later with a large silver key on an embroidered fob.

Reacher dropped the taxi guy, who bolted for the exit.

The manager moved closer. He held out the key, but before Reacher could take it, Nikki darted forward. She grabbed it. Walked to the doorway. Turned. Leaned against the frame. Stretched out her arm at shoulder height and dangled the key from her fingertips.

Nikki looked at Reacher and said, "Come."

He was halfway across the room before the word was out of her mouth. His duffel bag was in one hand. His stereo was in the other. He said, "Already there."

Silence fell on the room after Nikki and Reacher left, but it didn't last long. First, music started to play. Wailing guitar. Thundering bass and drums. Howling vocals. Then, another sound kicked in. It was just as rhythmic. *Thud. Thud. Thud.* And it was more relentless. It kept going and going. Another couple left the bar. *Thud. Thud. Thud.* Then, the final four slunk away. *Thud. thud. thud.* The noise upstairs got louder. The bartender felt like the walls were shaking. There was no sign of it slowing. No sign of it stopping. Not by the time the bartender finished cleaning and left the hotel. Not by the time the manager went home. Maybe it went on all night. The manager figured it could have because the door to room twelve was still locked the next morning when he knocked and tried the handle.

The clock in reception struck nine. Reacher and Nikki had not come downstairs. The clock struck ten. They had not emerged. It struck eleven. There was still no sign of them. Finally, the manager grabbed a passkey and crept back up the staircase. He knocked on the door again, louder this time. There was no reply. He tried the handle. The door didn't open. He worked the lock. He pushed. The door swung back but stopped after only an inch. The manager shoved as hard as he could, but he made no further progress. He peered through the narrow gap and saw something dark. It was made of wood. It was rough and unfinished. The back of the wardrobe. The big guy must have pushed it in front of the door. Which he could only have done from the inside.

The manager called out, "Hello? Room twelve? Anybody there?"

He got no reply. He pressed one ear close to the gap and prayed for the sound of a voice, or breathing, or groaning—anything to indicate life. He heard nothing.

The manager made his way slowly back down to the reception desk and picked up the phone. He dialed a one. Then another one. Then he dropped the receiver back into its cradle. He'd been thinking murder/suicide or drug overdose. Either way, a job for the police. But another thought had popped into his head. A distant recollection of something the hotel owner had told him, years ago, about why they should never put guests in room twelve. The details were hazy but it had to do with the people who owned one of the apartments in the adjoining building. About them making porno movies there and having weakened a section of the interconnecting wall in case they ever got raided and needed to get away. Apparently, they paid for the room to be left empty. He remembered wondering if they used cash or dirty video tapes as currency. And then he remembered a number they were supposed to call if the emergency exit from the apartment ever got used. It was disguised as a twenty-four-hour taxi contact on a card stuck inside one of the desk drawers. He found it, lifted the receiver again, and this time put it back down without dialing a single digit. He hadn't seen inside the room. He didn't know for sure that the neighbor's escape route had been used. He didn't know what would happen if he revealed he'd allowed room twelve to be used for no reason. He didn't know exactly, but he was certain it would be bad.

The manager rounded up the bellhop and the maintenance man, and between them they shoved the door far enough open for a person to squeeze through. He waited until the others were safely downstairs then eased himself through the gap. He saw the woman's boots and skirt and blouse lying on the floor next to the man's duffel. It was open and empty. His stereo was there, still plugged into the wall. The bed had been shoved aside. A cold chisel was on the floor, along with a rubber-wrapped club hammer. And a section of wall was missing. It was about four feet square, and ragged strips of wallpaper were hanging down in front of it. It was the emergency exit from the porn studio. Only the pair from the night before had used it as an entrance. They must have gone in that way and then let themselves out through the apartment's regular door. Presumably it was easier to open from the inside than the outside. The manager's head was full of questions. How had they known the wall had been weakened? Why had they gone through? What did they want? Maybe they'd been in a movie that was filmed there and went back to rob the place. Of money, or camera equipment, or unreleased videos. Or maybe they'd been ripped off and were looking to even the score. Maybe they were rivals, wanting to rid themselves of the competition. But whatever the reason, he knew what he had to do next. Call the number on the card in the drawer. Take the consequences. And pray they wouldn't be too awful.

The manager made it halfway to the door, then stopped. He'd never been on a porn set before. He couldn't help wondering what it would be like. So he turned back. Approached the hole in the wall. Knelt down. Crawled forward. Poked his head through the strips of paper. And immediately vomited. He was looking into a living room. It was sparsely furnished. There was a couch, with a briefcase propped up at one end. Two chairs. A coffee table. And three dead bodies.

Two of the bodies were male. Midtwenties, stocky, with square, shaved heads. The other was female. She had short, dark hair, and a blond wig had somehow gotten tangled around her right ankle.

Joe Reacher had read his people's unofficial reports by the time he caught up with his brother Jack on the phone.

"Any problems?" Joe said.

"None. Piece of cake."

"Sergeant Young, too? Nikki?"

"She enjoyed herself. Those KGB guys didn't know what hit them. And it's good to have gotten Hunt back in one piece."

"It sure is. And thanks for helping out. I had no one who could do what I needed."

"No problem. When will we know if it worked?"

"Couple of days. The medal ceremony. If O'Neill shows up, we're screwed."

Two days later, Adam O'Neill was waiting in an anteroom to the side of St. George's Hall in the Grand Kremlin Palace, Moscow. His time had finally come. He was minutes away from being officially named a Hero of the Soviet Union. His hair was freshly cut. He was wearing a new suit. Not the brash, gaudy kind that are cherished in the west. His outfit was honest and down-to-earth, such as someone like Tolstoy would have worn.

O'Neill pictured himself after the ceremony, walking through Red Square or strolling along the bank of the Moskva, with the five-pointed gold star pinned proudly to his chest. Such a simple symbol. But so elegant. So powerful. He would be the first American-born person ever to receive it. He could hardly believe the company he was about to keep. Zhukov. Brezhnev. Gagarin. Timoshenko . . .

"Comrade!" A man's voice snapped O'Neill out of his daydream.

The man who had spoken was small and wiry. He was in his fifties. His hair was short and tidy, and he was wearing a nondescript gray suit. He looked like a bank clerk, O'Neill thought, although he knew who the man was. Ilya Safonov. The second most senior officer in the KGB.

O'Neill snapped to attention. "Sir."

Safonov smiled. "No, no, no. There's no need for such formality. Not on such a special day. I just dropped by to give you this."

He took an envelope from his inside jacket pocket and held it out.

O'Neill said, "What is it, sir?"

"Go ahead. Take it. Open it."

O'Neill did as he was told. The envelope had been addressed by hand in old-fashioned, flowing script. It said, *Comrade O'Neill—"Hero" of the Soviet Union.* Inside there was a single piece of paper, folded three times. O'Neill flattened it out. It was a form made up of all kinds of boxes, printed in red with CCCP embossed at the top. Each box had a printed title, and each had been filled in by hand in blue ink. There were only two words he could understand. His first and last names. Then something drew his attention back to the envelope. To the quotation marks. He suddenly felt like his stomach had been hollowed out and replaced with a bucket of red-hot coals.

"You don't know what that is, do you?" Safonov said.

O'Neill didn't reply. He couldn't. There were so many thoughts whirling around his head that he was unable to form any words.

"Let me help you." Safonov smiled again, but this time without the slightest warmth. "Soon after you defected, another American soldier made contact. He said he wanted to come over to us, as well. He claimed he also had information to bring. Valuable information. We evaluated it, naturally, just as we did with yours. Care to guess what we found?"

O'Neill shook his head. His mouth was too dry to speak.

"A large part overlapped with yours. It matched. Exactly."

O'Neill managed, "That's good, right? Shows both sets of papers are genuine."

Safonov's smile faded into a scowl. "It shows the opposite. You see this man, a Major Hunt, was snatched back by the Americans before he could be exfiltrated. Or at least that's what they wanted us to think. The whole thing was a setup. A clumsy one. And they left this for us to find."

Safonov slid something else out of his pocket. A photograph. It was of the couch in the safe house in Mainz. Hunt's briefcase was sitting there, tucked safely in the corner.

O'Neill said, "I don't get it. What's the problem?"

"They left the briefcase. They wanted us to find it. And the papers that were in it. Which means the papers are bogus. They match your papers. So yours are also bogus."

"No. That's not true. My information is—"

"Disregarded. As are you. Hero, my ass. That paper I gave you? It's the official record of your conviction. We considered execution but decided that was too lenient. No, my son. You're going to Siberia. For the rest of your life. But if it's any consolation, that won't be very long."

DAVE BRUNS

GIVIN THE DOG A BONE

The dog had seen better days. Carl Boyd grew up on a farm. He knew dogs. This one looked like there was mastiff somewhere in the line, big frame, but his ribs were prominent through thin, patchy fur. He'd been hanging around Carl's remote desert adobe for five days now, never approaching Carl, but every morning the food Carl put out for him was gone. He'd seen dogs like this before, escapees from the small-town life of Malagua, the nearest city, or abandoned by their owners when times got tough or the dog got to be an inconvenience. They scratched out a meager existence in the arid countryside until they came up on the short end of a battle with coyotes or ended up grease spots on County Road 27 after tangling with a semi. Dog appeared to be about two years old, and from the looks of him, the prospects of seeing three were slim.

Today the mutt had come as close to Carl as he had yet. Carl sat quietly in a battered lawn chair, watching, not motioning for the dog to come, not calling him. Just watching. And the dog was curious. He knew Carl was his meal ticket for the future, but right now he was fixed for food for a few days. Carl knew this because the dog was close enough for Carl to see the hand and short expanse of ulna bone that the dog was carrying in his mouth. That hand had recently been attached to a living human, and that human was out there in the desert somewhere, although the living part of the equation was in question. Carl figured he should follow the dog and find the body, do whatever needed doing.

"Hey, babe," he called back into the house, "I may have to leave for a little bit. It's about the dog!"

"The dog is going to kill you and eat you one day, Carl. You need to leave him alone. Maybe he's rabid!"

Her voice. Three years together, and he still got shivers when he heard it. She'd proved tougher than he ever thought, accepted his need to fly dangerously, his smuggler life, and even saved that life one day in a memorable showdown with a psychopath bent on killing Carl. He figured she could handle a dog living with her if it came to that.

"I don't think eating me is high on his agenda right now. He's busy eatin' someone else." He heard the door slam behind him, then a small gasp as she realized what she was seeing.

"Oh, shit, Carl, what are we going to do?"

"*We* aren't doing anything. *I* am going to try and follow him when he leaves. He'll go back to the body because he knows there's food there."

As if on cue, the dog spun around and trotted toward the road and the trackless desert beyond. Carl checked the Colt Model 1911 holstered on his side and headed for his Jeep. He had to keep the dog in sight, and it might not be easy. The dog could go places even the Jeep couldn't, but so far, he seemed content to travel at a reasonable pace across level ground. Carl followed, keeping the Jeep in a low gear. If the mutt kept moving in the same direction, he'd be in rocky terrain within a couple miles or so; not mountains, or even hills, but a boulder-strewn area used as a resting spot by coyotes. The human kind. Carrying drugs or ferrying illegals across the desert. The hand might belong to a border jumper or a coyote, but whoever it was, they were almost certainly not innocent folks out for a drive through the desert.

The dog had slowed even more, leisurely now in the increasing heat of the late morning. Carl was approaching the first set of boulders, and the dog had just disappeared behind them. The desert was open and level on the other side, so Carl figured he could pick up the dog again after he negotiated the Jeep through the tangle of rock. He wasn't prepared for what he saw.

The crumpled remains of a Cessna Skylane 182 lay scattered across the desert floor, a wing here, wheels over there. Carl knew the plane although he'd never flown them, not when he flew for Air America, not running guns for FARC rebels, not flying weed for Marty Nelson back in the day. The plane was a popular model in the US, though, readily available, easy to fly, and featuring enough power and space for cargo, legitimate or otherwise.

He approached the downed plane slowly, hand on the Colt .45, his companion since he left Thailand back in 1973. Movement on his left and the gun cleared the holster. The big dog stood there, the hand still firmly clenched in his jaws. *Proud*, thought Carl. *He brought me here on purpose, wants to show me his find.*

A quick survey of the area convinced Carl there was no one else around, so he made his way to the fuselage, standing upright, nose down, as if someone had hammered it into the hard-packed earth. Somewhere in there was a pilot, and that pilot was missing a hand. At least. A peek inside the shattered right-side window revealed only a jagged piece of the plane's aluminum skin, impaled in the fabric of a seat, obscuring the view of the pilot. Carl guessed the force of the impact had driven the metal right through the arm of the pilot, leaving a stump attached to a pilot on one side and an irresistible treat for a dog on the other.

He worked his way around the monolith of the fuselage, cautious, watching for any sign that it might topple. Reaching the left side of the aircraft, he ducked under a severed strut and gazed through the broken glass. Just a pilot. A dead pilot missing his right hand. A dead pilot surrounded by more money than Carl had ever seen at one time in his life. Loose bills, mostly hundreds, littered the plane. Bundles of wrapped cash that had survived intact lay in profusion against the backs of the front seats. The rear seats and everything else in the plane's interior had been removed to limit weight and create additional space for cargo. And Carl knew what the cargo had been. Drugs, probably cocaine, one way, cash payments the other. Smuggler plane, with a pilot on the payoff run.

Carl gave the upright tube of metal a hard push, decided it wasn't going to fall on him, and, with some effort and screeching of metal, pulled the door open until he could get to the pilot. The body was pliable, no rigor, meaning the crash had occurred within the last few hours. No one was missing the plane or the pilot yet. The man's head was turned away, a large flap of skin torn back, revealing part of his skull. The body was still belted in the seat, and it took a moment for Carl to turn the man's face toward him, but when he saw it, he stopped, shocked. Even covered in dirt and crusted blood, Carl knew that face. Andrew Toomey, a chopper pilot from Nam.

Carl stepped away from the plane, sat on a nearby boulder, and recalled Toomey from the old days. A good pilot, too good to make any simple error. Toomey was never a straight arrow, but he hadn't been an outlaw either. He'd bend rules, take shortcuts, but never fell in with Carl or the black marketers Carl flew for in Laos and Cambodia. Apparently, he, like Carl, found the lure of easy money and the rush of dangerous flying too hard to resist on his return to civilian life.

How in the world did Toomey crash out here on a perfectly level desert on a still day with unlimited visibility? It made no sense. Could have been a mechanical thing, but planes were simple machines. Reliable. Nearly all plane accidents involved some level of pilot error. Toomey was one of the best pilots Carl ever knew, not a guy who would make those errors.

Carl's curiosity was piqued now, and he completed a cycle around the fuselage, then walked to where the wings landed after separating from the body. Coiled around a wing and trailing off into the desert was a length of half-inch steel cable. Carl hadn't flown this model, but he'd flown dozens of other small planes. The cable was not part of the aircraft. Had Toomey hit a power line, maybe a stabilizing cable for a telephone pole? No telephone poles out here, not for miles in any direction. Carl's house didn't even have a phone.

Carl strode back toward the body of the plane, noticed the dog was sniffing at Toomey's body, now more accessible through the open door.

He no longer held the hand in his mouth; eaten and the bone buried was Carl's guess. He returned to the Jeep, got out a canteen of water from his emergency bag, and poured some into a bowl from his cooking kit. He sat it down a ways off and watched. The dog lost interest in Toomey and cautiously approached the water, one eye on Carl ten feet away. Convinced that Carl meant him no harm, he turned his attention to the bowl and slurped up the entire contents before lying down in the shade of the Jeep.

Carl shut the plane's door to discourage the dog's future attempts to eat Toomey and turned back to the cable, following it for about a hundred yards. Two parallel outcroppings of rock thrust up from the ground, fifty yards apart here, and looking at one of them, Carl knew what happened. Someone had drilled deep into the rock, screwed a heavy eyebolt into place, and attached one end of the cable to it. Carl was pretty sure the other rock held a similar bolt and that the cable had been strung between the two by someone. Someone who knew where Toomey would be flying, who knew he'd be flying low, who knew he'd fly between these two outcroppings to throw off radar. When the propeller hit the cable, the plane would lose any ability to maneuver, and, that close to the ground, Toomey would have had no time to do anything but offer a brief prayer for his soul. He had died within seconds.

Only one reason to go to these lengths to drop a plane. Or perhaps one million reasons. Somebody was coming for the money. And Carl wanted to know who. He had been out of the game for a year; he'd had some close calls and had enough money to live on for now without running the risks anymore. But he still knew the people who knew the people, and the person who knew more of them than anyone was Tico. And Tico's bar was Carl's next stop. He hated to leave that kind of money but taking it without knowing who might come looking was a dicey proposition.

He fished his keys from the pockets of his khakis and walked back toward the Jeep. The dog saw him approaching and scampered away, ever watchful. Carl paused for a minute to see if the dog would come closer, but the mutt hadn't survived this long by being trusting. Carl nodded. "See ya around, buddy." The dog took another step back, so Carl turned the key and headed for Malagua.

The dog watched the man leave, peering out from between two rocks. He'd known men before. They had kicked him, beaten him, goaded him into fights with others like him. He remembered long hours on a heavy chain staked to the ground. Sometimes the men would come with thundersticks and point them at other dogs. The sticks would make a loud noise, and the dogs would fall, stop moving. When a man removed his chain one day, the dog saw his chance, broke away from the man and ran for the cover of the desert sage behind the place where the man lived. He heard the roar of the thunderstick, saw smoke, and felt the sting of hard bits of sand near his feet. And then he was free, couldn't see the man anymore.

The man who followed him here was different from the others. The dog wasn't sure if the food the man put out every night was meant for him, but the man wasn't angry that he ate it, in fact, put out more. And water, harder to find in the desert than food. The man had a thunderstick, the dog had seen it in his hand, but he never used it even though he had opportunities. The man was quiet, didn't yell or throw things at him. The dog was a survivor but knew he couldn't live out here forever. There were predators that crawled, slithered, and ran, competed for the little food that the desert offered. The man had given him a lifeline so far. The dog just wasn't sure yet if he could trust him. He watched the man's machine disappear in the distance, then turned and trotted back to the shade of the boulders.

Tico's was a Malagua institution and Tico a local icon. A bar owner, philanthropist, font of wisdom, and voracious reader of detective fiction, Tico was, more than any of these, a money launderer. The bar was a gold mine, but the income from the raucous weekend partiers and steady tourist dinner trade paled next to the money Tico made washing dirty cash for numerous nefarious enterprises from El Paso to San Antonio. Carl knew that Tico never shied from violence, had a history in the drug trade in Mexico, had seen men killed and had killed men himself. Aging now, he continued to be a fearsome adversary to his en-emies and a good friend to Carl.

"And the money is still there, Carl? In the desert?"

"Right in the plane where I found it. Toomey was too good a pilot to make a mistake. Probably flew this route clean before, had no reason to be concerned. No, the cable was put there on purpose. Three forces at work here, Tico. They all want the money. Number one, the guys who lost it. Number two, the guys who stretched that cable. Number three, me. I need to know who the other guys are."

Tico stroked his chin thoughtfully. "This intrigues me, Carl. I have heard of it before. Years ago, in Mexico. You have heard me speak of my daughter and her death?"

Carl had, but Tico had never revealed details, only that he left the drug trade afterward. The rest was a mystery.

"My daughter was a bright light in a dark world. She could have been anything she chose to be, would have made a difference. But like so many young people, she went through a rebellious stage. She took up with a very bad man, a gringo, a competitor. I think she believed that her romance with him might bring peace between that man and me, settle disputes we had over territory. But she was young, naive. The man used her as a bludgeon to try to force me to give him my routes, my buyers. My pride was too great, and I refused. So he had her killed to punish me. Aiden Knopfler."

The name meant nothing to Carl. Not someone in the trade any-more, he was sure of that. But Tico was still talking, and Carl refocused.

"I found the men who killed my daughter. Each of them died in a terrible way. But not Knopfler. I destroyed his business, killed his men, but Knopfler himself escaped, went into hiding. He began to use his knowledge of the trade to look for easy scores, stealing drugs or cash from growers and wholesalers. And once, I heard of this same practice, this cable bringing down a low-flying plane loaded with cash, south of Juarez. It was Knopfler, I was certain. My efforts to follow the trail, how-ever, were futile. The man was a ghost. And now I get, perhaps, another chance at the man who took what I loved most."

One force accounted for. The man who killed Toomey. And Tico's daughter. The remaining question was whose money did Knopfler take?

"After all this time, eh? Maybe this is your chance? If you're with me here, we have a lot of reasons to get back to that plane. Any idea who the money belongs to?"

"This is also something I know. This man, Toomey, flies, or flew, cocaine for Arturo Dominguez. Dominguez operates out of Terlingua, practically owns Terlingua. He will not be pleased. If he knows Toomey is down, he may already be on his way there, and he'll bring an army for that much money. If we want the money, we need to return soon. Knopfler is likely to be there soon as well. If he knows Toomey's route, he must have a source in Dominguez's operation. As you said, Carl. Three forces about to meet in the desert. Very Clint Eastwood, do you agree?" Tico was smiling but his eyes had a fierce light in them that wouldn't be extinguished until Knopfler died by his hand.

"I will notify my men, Carl, and we should be on the road in half an hour. I hope we arrive in time."

Carl walked to the Jeep and was soon joined by Tico and his two lieutenants. In all the years Carl had known them, he had never learned their names, just called them "the Desperados." They rarely spoke, and their looks alone were usually sufficient to calm the rowdier elements at Tico's bar. Today both were armed with revolvers and razor-sharp knives. Tico carried no visible weapon, and Carl hoped none of them would need one. Hard to believe Tico would settle for anything short of a fatal confrontation with Knopfler, though. If it came to that, it wouldn't be Carl's first. The Desperados piled into Tico's ancient Land Rover, Carl pulled out, and the little caravan headed for the desert.

Four hours had passed since the dog led Carl to the downed plane. A lot could happen. Carl was hoping to find the site undisturbed as he had left it. He didn't. Found, instead, a massacre, bodies strewn throughout the rocks, swatches of blood soaking into the desert floor. The two vehicles stopped well short of the scene, the Desperados exiting and surveying the area. No sign of life. Certainly not among the broken and bleeding bodies on the sand. Tico and Carl held a brief conference.

Tico pointed. "Dominguez. The one with the boots."

Carl turned his head, saw the nearest body was wearing custom-made boots with the stylized letters *AD* carved on the sides in bloodred dye. Toomey's employer. No sign of the men who had killed him.

"The rest?" he asked Tico, hand sweeping to indicate the other bodies.

"Soldiers. I believe they all belong to the Dominguez organization. Ambushed, it appears. The world will survive without their presence. I suspect it will be a better place. More so, if this was the work of Knopfler and I can find him. But I fear he has taken the money and is long gone by now."

"I can answer that question easily enough, Tico." Carl began to pick his way through the rocks toward the plane, leaving Tico and the Desperados to search the bodies for any sign of what happened.

The plane was right where Carl had left it; Toomey hadn't gone anywhere, nor had his cargo. A million dollars, maybe more. *Why would someone ambush the owners, then leave a million dollars on the table?* Carl heard the shots then, two so close they almost sounded like one, and he knew the answer. Knopfler had seen them coming, didn't have time to get the money out of the plane, and had set up a second ambush instead. Carl pulled the Colt, cocked it, began working his way back through the boulders.

Two new bodies added to the slaughter on the other side. One Desperado and one man Carl didn't know. The Desperado was alive, seated on the ground, his left arm limp, bleeding. His Smith and Wesson .44 lay near the now useless hand. The stranger was clearly dead. The Desperado won the battle, but Knopfler was winning the war. Two more men with guns. One stood with a rifle pointed at the remaining Desperado while the other held his pistol to Tico's head. He was the one who spoke.

"You need to drop that gun, friend, or Tico here gets his brain spattered all over this boulder."

Carl hesitated only a second. There was no plausible scenario where he could take out the two gunmen without Tico and the Desperados dying in a hail of gunfire. He let the Colt slip carefully from his hand.

"Carl, this is Senor Knopfler. I believe I have mentioned him."

"I'm sure you have, Tico," Knopfler cut in. "To many people. And to no purpose. You never got any of them to give me up, and here we are again with me holding the upper hand. Does the losing get old, Tico? Losing your business, losing your daughter, losing out on the money here? Of course, I lost out on your daughter, too. Enjoyed my time with her, but, hey, all good things, eh?"

Carl could see the tension in Tico, the readiness to move. Prayed that Knopfler would continue gloating long enough for Carl to think of something, anything, to turn the tables. But Knopfler had ended his speech. Carl gauged the distance to the second gunman—too far. One Desperado incapacitated, the other certain to die along with Tico as soon as Knopfler pulled the trigger. But Knopfler didn't pull the trigger.

The dog heard the men coming long before he saw them, crept back into an old coyote den under a rock and watched them arrive. Instinct told him these men weren't like the one who fed him. Three came, then six more. The first three had climbed into the boulders above the dog and hid there, just as the dog had hidden from them. Each carried a thunderstick, some long, some short, but the dog knew that any of them could make him fall and never rise. He shrunk farther back into the den.

The new arrivals left their travel machine and fanned out looking for something, maybe the dead man in the metal tube. Before they reached the boulders, the thundersticks above exploded, men falling like the dogs in Malagua had. Soon, all six lay sprawled on the ground, motionless. The dog stayed still and silent. The men would have no interest in him, so he had little interest in them.

He lay in the den for what seemed like a lifetime as the three men gathered thundersticks from the other six, poking and prodding their bodies, searching their travel machine. Then the sound of another travel machine, new men coming, caused the three to retreat to the boulders again. Two machines, four more men now. But the dog knew one of these men. The man who fed him. Gave him water. The quiet man who watched him and followed him. His ears raised, and the hackles along his back followed suit. Now he was interested.

Then more thunder, two men falling. The food-man had disappeared, but his friends were now in front of the den, the men with the thundersticks standing with their backs to the hidden dog, ready to make them fall. Then the food-man reappeared, laying his thunderstick down. Two of the other men were speaking to each other, but the dog knew they were not friends. The talk was harsh, their movements those of anger and aggression. He eased himself out of the den, staying in the shadow, his back to the rock.

Knopfler couldn't imagine a better scenario. The plane went down perfectly according to plan, he was able to eliminate Dominguez, and now his longtime nemesis, the man who caused him to move from house to house, city to city, always looking over his shoulder for more than a decade, was at his mercy and about to die. Oh, yeah, and he was going to be a million dollars richer. He raised the gun to Tico's head and spoke his final words: "I kinda miss your daughter, Tico, but I won't miss you!"

He never saw it coming, just felt the searing pain as the dog's jaws clamped down on his wrist; felt the hand with the gun dropping toward the ground, away from its intended target; felt the shot meant for Tico rip through his own foot. Carl's world suddenly became very busy. Knopfler's partner spun away from the Desperado he was holding at gunpoint and tried to get a clean shot at the dog who was shaking Knopfler's arm like a chew toy. He fired once, and the dog yelped, released Knopfler's arm, headed for the safety of the boulders. Gone. In one smooth, practiced motion, Tico dropped to a squat, pulled a hidden ankle gun from its webbing, rose, and shot Knopfler at point-blank range. One in the chest, the second in the throat. Carl had a brief window to act, and he took advantage. He fell flat, scrabbling for the still-cocked Colt, found it, rolled, and squeezed off round after round. Most missing but enough hitting the second gunman that he was dead before Carl emptied the magazine.

The world retreated then. Slowed to a crawl. Carl's hearing grudgingly returned; his vision, obscured by smoke and grit, cleared. Two men left standing. Desperado One was bent over Desperado Two, tending to his wound. Tico stood over Knopfler.

"Is he dead, Tico?"

"Not yet. Soon. But he is dead to me. My revenge is complete. I feel no better, though perhaps relieved my search is over. It does nothing to fill the empty place inside me." And he turned away from Knopfler and walked toward the Cessna.

Carl stood, brushed off the sand, and followed the path the dog had taken into the cover of the boulders. No sign. Some blood smeared on a rock but Carl didn't know if it was Knopfler's or the dog's. Not much else to do. If the dog was hit, he wouldn't last long out here; if he wasn't, well, maybe they'd meet again. Carl joined the others hauling money from the plane.

A week passed. A Border Patrol agent named Stouffer, driven by curiosity about hovering vultures in an area frequented by illegals, found three trucks, ten dead bodies, and the remains of an airplane in what appeared to be a drug deal gone bad. Hard to tell what happened. Looked like the plane crashed, then everybody just shot each other. One guy shot himself in the foot. Maybe somebody got away with the dope since Stouffer couldn't find any. He reported it, an investigation was completed, and the conclusion was that there would never be an accurate conclusion. Ten bad guys dead. If some bad guys got away, well, Border Patrol didn't need to be greedy.

For his part, Carl lay low, didn't go to town, didn't see Tico. Explained everything to her.

"Thought we were past all that, Carl? Thought you were done."

"A million dollars, babe. And I didn't plan on this, just walked in on it trying to help someone. And Tico finally gets a little peace."

"True. And I do love Tico. He's the reason I came back to you in the first place. Can't say I'm happy about it, but I can see you didn't have much choice. We need to have everyone over, talk through this, and make sure it doesn't come back on anyone. We'll grill burgers and corn. I'll fix a nice salad."

"We found a million dollars, sweetheart. We'll grill T-bones."

They met, talked about alibis, deniability. Commiserated with the wounded Desperado and his wife who had to take care of him. Divvied up the money, equal shares for each of the four after medical expenses for the wounded Desperado. Nearly a quarter mill each. Carl grilled steaks, the men drank whiskey, the women wine. At dark, they moved the party inside while Carl remained on the patio cleaning up. She noticed he was taking a long time to clear a few dishes and scrub the grill. They had guests, the first time ever. She hated the reason but loved the people. She was the perfect hostess, but Carl needed to get back inside and do his host duties. She went to the back door, shouted through the screen.

"Hey, Carl, get your butt in here—everybody's waiting to talk to you!"

"Yeah, just a minute, babe. I'll be right in, but there's a hero layin' out here on the patio. He's back and he's OK. I'm just givin' the dog a bone."

TORI ELDRIDGE

ROCK AND ROLL AIN'T NOISE POLLUTION

Candace leaned into the Neumann TLM microphone and dropped her voice to an intimate, yet intense, level—one-on-one, coach to player—as if millions of people weren't listening to her across the country. "If you want your boss to treat you like a valuable part of his team, you have to fight smarter."

"But how?" the caller whined, voice squeaking like the wheels of Candace's old sound-booth chair.

If WD-40 worked on vocal cords, Candace would have bought the whole supply and mailed it to every member of her audience—or, better yet, hired some tech genius to invent a whine-reducing, phone-transmitted technology her producer could blast during caller screening. How brilliant would that be? Her callers would be one step closer to empowerment before they even said hello. And Candace would be one step farther from losing her shit on the air.

"Well, to begin with, stop reacting emotionally. No quivering lip, no snarky retorts, no heaving sighs. Look him square in the eyes, drop your voice an octave, and respond to the issue at hand. Not the delivery, not the attitude, not even the word choice. Speak about the issue."

"But I did," the caller whined again, this time rising to the frequency of a petulant teen.

Shoot me now.

Candace clenched the edge of her console. If it were humanly possible, she'd jump through the microphone and throttle the whine right out of her caller's voice. Hadn't the woman been listening? Or did she actually believe she sounded like a confident, capable adult? Either possibility made Candace's head throb. These days, every show ate another layer of her patience. Pretty soon there'd be nothing left.

She took a breath to speak. Then didn't. She had said all there was to say. She didn't trust herself to repeat it, again.

She gazed at her producer through the soundproof glass, shrugged innocently, and hit the drop button. "Uh-oh. I think we lost our caller."

Neil gave her the first scolding look of the day.

"Guess she drove through a bad cell zone." Candace smirked. "Remember, callers, landlines are best. Who do we have next, Neil?"

"Susan from Van Nuys. On a *land*line."

Candace mouthed, *Ha ha*, then flipped the switch for line two. "Hello, Susan, welcome to *Stone Cold Truth*. What's troubling you today?"

"Hi, Doctor Stone. Thanks so much for taking my call. How are you?"

Candace dropped her face in her hands. Every call began in the same chatty way, as if they were best friends who hadn't talked in ages and had all the time in the world to catch up with the latest gossip. And each time, Candace answered with the same response: "Fine, Susan. But how are *you*?"

"Um, not so good. It's just like when I was a kid . . ."

Candace muted her microphone and groaned.

"Don't even think about dropping this call," Neil said, speaking over Susan's woeful tale. He had switched his microphone from the broadcast feed to the private line he used to prompt Candace with facts or warn her when a commercial break approached. Now, he was just being a jerk. Bad enough she had to listen to this caller vomit her childhood before getting to the point, now she had Neil scolding her like a child?

"Susan, let's leave your childhood in the past and jump ahead to why you're calling me today."

"Oh, right. Sorry about that, I just wanted to give you some history, you know? Like when I was fourteen . . ."

"Don't do it," Neil warned as Candace reached for the drop button.

She clenched her fingers and pulled them back. He was right. Rambling stories and whining voices went part and parcel with the job and, honestly, were her show's greatest appeal. Desperate callers reminded her audience they weren't alone in their struggles and gave them a chance to receive advice without putting themselves on the line. It gave them the confidence to tackle the day and feel good about themselves.

At least, that was the theory. These days, Candace wondered if she was making any impact at all. Oh, people were listening, all right, but were they really hearing what she had to say?

The caller's voice droned in the background, something about Harry and leaving and—a dog? Candace was finding it harder and harder to pretend she cared. It wasn't as if she could actually solve the woman's problems in one phone call. The woman had to know that, right? She had to know this was just feel-good radio entertainment.

A sequence of pops made Candace jump.

She shouldn't have heard any outside noises because the walls of her sound booth were thick, and the windows—one facing Neil's control room and the other facing the hallway—were made of laminated studio glass.

Where was Neil?

Candace craned her neck but didn't see him anywhere near the console. She looked out the observation window and checked the hallway. Everything seemed quiet out there.

"Susan, are you on a cell phone outside?"

"Oh no, Doctor Stone. I've been listening to you for years. I know how you feel about callers on cell phones. So, like I was saying . . ."

As Susan continued to relay her story, Candace turned down the volume. She didn't need to hear the details, only enough of Susan's voice to know she was still talking. That way, Candace could dive into the gap with some innocuous comment and improvise the rest. In the meantime, she could have a private conversation with her missing producer.

She switched her microphone from broadcast to control. "Neil, can you hear me? What's going on out there?" When he didn't answer, she leaned over her desk so she could check the entrance to his control room and found him standing in the doorway, looking around the bend.

A sound exploded like a firecracker through her headphones. Then two more, in quick succession.

Candace tore off her headphones and pressed her hands against her ears, trying to relieve the pain of the sound broadcasted through Neil's microphone.

Her window shook. Neil pounded on the glass from the hallway, his face contorted with fear. He yelled, "Gun. Get out," loud enough to carry up the hallway, into the control room, through his still hot microphone, and out of the headphones Candace was holding. Then he ran.

Oh my god, oh my god, oh my god. This can't be happening.

Candace scrambled under the console, shaking as she pulled in her chair for cover.

Cover? What a joke. The heavy wood sides of the console offered nothing more than concealment. But that should be enough, right? The shooter wouldn't waste a bullet on furniture if he didn't think anyone was in the studio. Or would he?

She grabbed the headphones, stretched the cord to its limit, and flipped one of the cans so she could press it against her ear.

People screamed. Doors slammed. Another gunshot fired.

Candace yelped and pulled away, clutching her head to stop the memories.

No, no, no. Not again.

She covered her ears, shutting out the noise like the earmuffs she wore at the range. Those shots were good. These were bad. Like the shots fired that night in the West Hollywood clinic. The ones that stole the lives of two young men. The ones that caused her to shut down her practice, call in favors, and start anew. The ones that sent her to the firing range every Sunday morning for the last eleven years.

Candace leaned out from under the console. People ran past her window toward the stairway exit. Should she make a run for it too, or stay hidden? She couldn't decide. She could barely think. She, who had all the answers, couldn't make a simple decision.

She pressed the can to one ear and retreated back under the console as far as the cord would allow. The voice came through loud and clear. "I'm here for *you*, Doctor Stone. Come on out and give me some of your professional doctor advice."

The shooter was after her? Holy hell. Every muscle in her body screamed at her to bolt, but her logical mind held her fast. If she ran now, he'd gun her down. But if she stayed, she'd be trapped.

Or would she?

There was no way for him to know she was hiding in this particular studio. The building had five others on this floor and, since each studio was shared by multiple hosts, none of them had placards on the doors with show names and logos. Candace could be in any of them. Or she could have fled down the stairs with everyone else.

Gunshots fired.

Although the noise hurt, she kept the headphone pressed against her ear and stuffed down the rising panic.

It's not like before. Please, not like before.

A woman screamed, "Please don't—"

Another shot fired.

Candace stifled a cry.

She had to do something. But what?

Susan's murmuring voice escalated loud enough for Candace to hear despite the lowered volume. "Doctor Stone, are you still there?"

Because Neil had switched his microphone to a private line, the radio audience hadn't heard the gunshots coming through Candace's headphones.

"Well?" Susan asked. "What do you think I should do, stay or go?"

Candace scoffed. *Wasn't that the million-dollar question?*

"Come out, come out, wherever you are," the shooter sang in the distance. "I've got a friend of yours, or maybe she's an enemy. Which is it, lady? Did the great Doctor Stone ruin your life, too? Did she poison your mind like she poisoned my wife's? Fill your head with lies? Tell you to pack up and leave?"

A woman cried out, but anything she might have said afterward was too soft and far away to hear.

Candace crawled out from under the console, put on her headphones to free her hands, then peeked over the top to check the windows. No one in the hallway. She rose a little taller. No one in the control room, either. Although she was safe for the moment, if she reached across the console to her soundboard, she'd be in full view if the shooter appeared.

What good was being a life coach if she couldn't save a life?

"Doctor Stone? Are you even there?" Susan asked.

Candace reached over the console and hit the buttons to switch her microphone feed from control room to broadcast. "Yes, Susan, I'm here. But I have more pressing business at the moment, so I'm going to cut you off."

She killed Susan's line, upped the gain on her microphone, and knelt on the floor where she could talk within range without getting herself shot. "Listen up, audience, we have a shooter in the building, and I need someone out there to call 911. I'm at the Sound Path Recording building on the corner of De Longpre and St. Andrews, second floor. My producer left his microphone on and his door open, so I can hear some of what's going on out there."

A woman screamed.

"I need help, people. Most of my colleagues have left the building. I'm trapped in my sound booth. I don't know if anyone's been injured. As of a second ago, there was at least one other woman alive on this floor."

Candace took off her headphones and leaned around the side of the console. Although the hallway appeared to be empty, her field of vision was limited.

She reached across her soundboard and flipped a switch she had never used before—the one-way intercom connected to the hallway speakers on her floor. The system was intended for emergency use only— show emergencies, not shooter-in-the-building emergencies. But hey, a take-charge woman used whatever tools she had at hand, right? Wasn't that what she told her callers? *"Deal with things as they are, not as you want them to be, and the opportunities for success will appear."*

Candace put the headphones back on, knelt on the floor, and spoke loudly toward the microphone. "Don't hurt her. It's me you want. Isn't that what you said? You came here for me?" Her words projected through the hallway speakers, were picked up by Neil's microphone in the producer's booth, and fed back to Candace through her headphones, giving her the peculiar feeling of being in two places at once.

"Where are you?" the shooter yelled. He sounded close. Too close.

Candace crouched lower, tipping back her head to keep her mouth as high and in line with the microphone as she dared. "Talk to me. What's your name? What have I done to make you so angry?"

"Come and find out. Or do you need a life coach to tell you what to do? Is that it, Doc? Are you too chicken to face your own life? Is that why you stick your nose where it doesn't belong?"

His voice was growing louder, probably as he drew closer to Neil's microphone. She had to steer him away. "Your voice is getting softer. Speak up."

His laughter dripped with disdain. "Marco . . . Polo! Not so smart after all, are you, Doc? How's this? Can you hear me now? Am I speaking loud enough for you?" The rest of what he said was lost to the microphone as he walked in the other direction.

Candace took off the headphones, hurried to the window, and pressed her face against the glass. At the far end of the hall, the shooter—a short man with shaggy dark hair and paramilitary castoffs—shoved a woman Candace didn't recognize against the closed door of Studio Five. He motioned for her to open the door and when she couldn't, fired his pistol into the door's observation window.

Faint sounds of the shot and shattering glass carried through the headphones Candace had abandoned on the console. She could tell he was yelling, but she couldn't hear what he was saying.

Watch or listen? She couldn't do both.

Candace ran back to the console, flipped a can, and pressed it against her ear. The shooter was still yelling, but he was too far from Neil's microphone for her to discern the words. What if he was threatening to kill the woman? What if he was giving Candace some sort of ultimatum and she didn't respond?

"Tell me about your wife," she said, hoping to disrupt his tirade and redirect his rage back onto her. "You said I poisoned her mind. What did you mean by that?"

Although she could barely hear him, she couldn't tell him to speak up because he'd know he had moved farther away from her. Her best option was to keep him talking and hope he'd lose interest in the woman and let her go—or at the very least, not shoot her. The cops had to be on their way. Candace just needed to keep everyone alive until they arrived.

"But why do you think your wife called me?" she said, interrupting whatever he was saying.

Without waiting for an answer, Candace took off the headphones and raced to the window. The shooter was standing in the middle of the hallway now, pointing his pistol at the woman's temple and yelling up at a speaker. He must have thought it acted as a microphone and didn't realize the intercom system only went one way. He shoved the woman toward Studio Six—only two doors up on Candace's side of the hallway—and disappeared from sight.

Candace hurried back to the console and lunged over the side so she could reach the microphone faster. "I don't understand," she said, panting from the sudden exertion. "But I really want to. Maybe if I understood the situation better, I could help you get her back."

Candace had no idea whether her comments fit with what the shooter had been saying, but she knew from experience that people were less likely to act rashly when they were thinking and speaking.

She headed for the door that connected her sound booth to Neil's control room.

Smart move or a deadly mistake?

Only one way to find out.

She opened the door and was greeted by the muffled rant of the shooter. Was he still inside Studio Six? If so, that might give her a chance to escape.

Or she could find a weapon and take him on.

Candace had watched two people die in her former clinic. There was no way she'd let that woman die in this radio station.

Neil had left a gear bag under his desk, probably full of sweaty gym clothes—not much help unless Candace wanted to asphyxiate the shooter. Aside from that, the control room was bare: just the mixing console, a phone, a couple of chairs—and a putter. It leaned in the corner of the room beside an automated putting cup, the kind that kicked back the ball for another shot.

She grabbed the putter and went to the open hallway door. If she got out of this mess alive, she'd invite Neil to a round of golf at the exclusive Los Angeles Country Club, where her father had held membership for the last thirty years. Better yet, she'd buy him a new set of clubs.

Tomorrow. Please, God, let me see tomorrow.

"Where'd you go, Doc? I'm not good enough for you?" The shooter's voice grew louder and clearer. "You don't want to talk to me no more?" He was back in the hallway. But how close?

Candace cocked the putter over her shoulder like a bat and leaned against the hinges of the open door, grateful she was a lefty, but painfully aware that she wouldn't have room to swing. If she wanted to make use of this weapon, she'd have to take another risk. But wasn't that how you lived an empowering and fulfilling life? By taking risks? That's what she told her radio audience.

She peeked around the door in time to see the shooter shove his hostage into Studio Four—the one next to hers.

Candace ran up the hallway, ducking below the studio's sound-booth window, and dashed up the hallway past the open control room door.

"You hiding under there, Doc?" the shooter yelled from inside the sound booth.

The woman cried. Something thudded and crashed.

Studio Four aired the *Rock and Roll Ain't Noise Pollution* show, hosted by Raymond Getz. If the gunman had so much as scratched one of Angus Young's collectible Gibson SG guitars that hung on Ray's walls, the host would hold her responsible and kill her himself.

Not that it mattered. Her chances were next to nil to survive.

Candace switched her grip for a right-handed swing. Although it wouldn't be as powerful as swinging from the left, she could attack sooner. Was this the right strategy? Hell if she knew. In all her years doling out radio advice, Candace had never talked anyone through an active shooter crisis.

The hostage stumbled into the hallway as if she had been pushed out the control room door. A second later, the gun emerged. Candace swung the putter down on the shooter's wrist, knocking the pistol from his hand. He howled, but instead of going for the weapon, he came for her: too fast to swing again, too close to run, too sudden for her to do anything but get hit in the gut and tackled onto the floor.

Air whooshed from her lungs as his shoulder jammed into her diaphragm. He hit her, again and again, pain exploding across her face with each blow.

"What's the matter, Doc? Nothing to say?"

His hands clenched around her throat and slammed her head against the floor. The hallway went gray.

Don't black out. Don't black out.

She bent her knees, remembering a technique she had learned in a rape prevention seminar the month before, and thrust up her hips. If her attacker had been taller or heavier, it might not have worked. But the man was short and wiry, so he jolted forward and released her throat. Candace sucked in the air, rammed her knee into his coccyx, rolled off to the side, and crawled for the gun. It was only a couple yards away, but when he grabbed her ankle, it seemed like a mile.

"Wait," Candace yelled to the hostage, who bolted down the hallway and out the stairwell door. "Dammit!" She needed help getting that gun.

The shooter yanked on her ankle. She kicked with her free leg, hit nothing, then flipped onto her back and stomped. The man howled and released her ankle. Candace scrambled to her feet, scooped the gun off the floor—and tripped.

As her face headed for the floor, she tucked her shoulder and rolled. It wasn't pretty, and it wasn't smooth, but it gained her a few precious feet. Enough time to rise and turn.

Then, with the surety of 572 Sundays, she fired.

The man slowed, stumbled, and fell to his knees. His hands clutched his chest, and his brows furrowed with astonishment. He opened his mouth to speak, then crumpled onto the floor.

Candace shuddered and cried. And when she couldn't hear her own voice over the roaring in her ears from the gun, she sobbed.

Hands grabbed her arms and snatched the weapon. LAPD yelled commands and questions she couldn't understand. One officer, a woman with the kindest eyes she had ever seen, cupped Candace's face in her hands and spoke intently with what appeared to be questions.

Candace stared and strained.

The roaring receded.

"Are you okay, Doctor Stone? Are you hurt?"

"I, uh . . . No. I don't think so."

The officer nodded. "Good. You should sit down."

A chair had been rolled behind her. Once she saw it, her legs gave way and she sat. She focused on the officer's name tag. Cooper. It seemed like a nice name. A nice name for a nice person. Not someone trying to gun down a building full of innocent people.

Two sets of paramedics rolled gurneys past her up the hallway.

"Was anyone killed?"

"We don't know yet," Officer Cooper replied.

Candace sagged. "He was here for me."

"We know. The woman you rescued filled us in when we arrived. She said you saved her life."

Candace shook her head. "She wouldn't have been in danger if it weren't for me."

"True. But that doesn't discount what you did for her." Officer Cooper squeezed her hand. "Or what you did for me."

Candace looked at her—really looked at her—and saw in her expression something more than professional consideration. "I'm sorry.

I'm a little shaken right now, so I'm not thinking very clearly. Have we met?"

Officer Cooper shook her head. "Just on the phone. I was having a hard time a few years back, trying figure out what to do with my life. You helped me sort things through and gave me the courage to stand up to my folks and do what felt right for me."

"Law enforcement?"

"Uh-huh. I took the entrance exam a week after our conversation."

Candace nodded. "Yeah, it can happen that way. Decisions come pretty quick once you cut out the crap and lock onto what's important."

"Like how you saved that woman's life? He could have shot her any-time. You kept him engaged. Kept his anger focused on you."

Candace laughed and shook her head, not ready to admit to any-thing quite that grandiose.

She wasn't a cop or a soldier who put their lives on the line for others. And she certainly wasn't a hero. She was a life coach with a PhD in psychology. A talk-show host, armed with a microphone, a willing-ness to listen, and a fair amount of uncommon sense to share. If that was enough to inadvertently save a life, then great.

More than great. Worthy.

She had a platform that reached millions. She'd never take that for granted again. And no matter how long it took for her callers to share their stories, she'd stay with them and listen.

SANDRA BALZO

BACK IN BLACK

"They board as passengers, disembark as cargo," Leo muttered, watching the herd of diners move directly from the late dinner seating to the all-night buffet. All ages, they were, on this cruise. Ankle biters to retirees. Ankle biters *with* retirees.

He tossed his cigarette over the rail into the Tasman Sea. God, he was knackered.

Not easy being the prototypical Aussie for the five straight days and nights of the cruise across the ditch to Auckland. Leo much preferred his rainforest tour gig. There he could say and do what he wanted, take the bastards where he wanted.

Just then a woman with blond hair—a sheila, he'd say for the tourists, maybe throw in that she was going to put shrimp on the barbie—cut an older man and woman away from a group emerging from the dining room. The older woman was slow-walking as the blond talked at her, the man trailing behind them.

Leo sunk into the black of the overhang as they passed, not feeling sociable.

"—last chance tonight," the blond was saying. "Tomorrow we'll be docking."

"But . . . I'm just not sure."

The younger woman locked arms with her. "I'll walk with you."

"Please," the man said, touching the blond's arm. "I've cared for Hallie these last months, and, sure, there are times she wants to give up. When she feels she's a burden. But if she has changed her mind about this . . ."

They were past Leo now, moving through the muster station. No one went this way at night. Probably didn't like to be reminded that even a ship this size could sink, especially in the Tasman Sea, one of the world's roughest bodies of water.

Leo stuck his head out from his hidey-hole to see their silhouettes at the rail, shadowed by the lifeboats above. He could barely make out a taller figure now or . . . No, not taller, just higher. Climbing on the rail.

And then it was gone.

A splash.

"Hallie," the man's voice sobbed. "Please, somebody help her."

"You, then," the young woman's voice said. "You help her."

Another splash.

Silence for one, two, three, five, ten, twenty seconds, and then, finally, a high-pitched keening.

As Leo stepped from the shadows, the blond woman ran to him, tears streaming down her face.

———

"My god. I had no idea it would be so beautiful."

"Now why would that be?" Cate handed her new husband of exactly thirty-three days a glass of champagne as she joined him at the railing of the Daintree Rainforest Lodge. "I rambled on about it ad nauseam, according to you."

Cate pushed a lock of blond hair behind one ear and took a sip of her own champagne, marveling in the almost painfully green, ephemeral nature of the rainforest and the futility of the lodge's attempt to tame it. Even the frosted champagne glass she held was an illustration, the ice-bucket chill of the champagne clashing with the stifling heat and humidity. The rainforest would win as it always did, the champagne going tepid if left undrunk and the glass dripping a forlorn puddle onto the rail.

Sip now, or forever hold your peace.

"—have to look at it from my perspective," John was saying, swiping at his brow. "You wanted to travel nearly twenty hours to spend our slightly belated honeymoon in the Australian rainforest. A place that's in the southern hemisphere and two ticks away from the equator. And in January, which is the middle of their summer. Can you blame me for being hesitant?"

She opened her mouth to reply.

He held up his hand. "And the more I resisted, the more eloquent you became."

"Three thousand plant species, seventy-seven of them rare," Cate reminded him. "Not to mention twelve thousand different insect species—"

"But you did mention them," John said with a wry grin. "And that's all I heard: blah, blah, blah, heat. Blah, blah, bugs; blah, blah, blah, crocodiles. And, oh yeah, blah, blah, snakes."

"Because you have selective hearing," Cate said with a grin. "I think I told you that the night we met."

A meeting facilitated by one of those dating services that checks your net worth before lifting a hand to help you meet the man or woman of your dreams.

"But you must admit," she continued, "that it is beautiful. And unique. And half the cost in the summer, which is their 'wet season.'"

"Wet season, in a rainforest, imagine that. But neither of us needs to worry about money." He slipped his arm around her waist. "I just want to be sure you're all right staying here, given what happened two years ago."

"Absolutely," she said, lifting her chin. "This lodge holds my last happy memory with my parents. We spent a week here and then boarded a cruise ship in Cairns for Auckland. My parents had such fun." She giggled. "I have to admit, I barely saw them onboard. They insisted on the full cruise experience, which wasn't my thing at all. Dressing for dinner, going to shows, the captain's table and all. I thought, let them enjoy it, and then we'll explore New Zealand together. What I didn't know was that my mother was dying and had other plans."

Cate's mother had taken her own life, climbing over the rail and into the sea on the last night of the cruise. Her stepfather had drowned in an attempt to save her.

"I was traumatized," she admitted. "In fact, I came back here to the lodge until the search for their bodies was called off, and I was finally allowed to leave the country."

"What a nightmare for you," John said, covering her hand with his. "The memories have to be—"

"But that's what I'm saying. The memories here in the rainforest are all lovely." She turned her hand over to lace her fingers through his. "I came to terms with my mother's decision. She found her peace, and I . . . well, I guess I found mine here." She forced a laugh. "I must have been quite the Debbie Downer, though, sitting in my black linen dress under the ceiling fans." She gestured to the enormous wooden blades rotating overhead.

"And I think it's nice here this time of year. Fewer people, more . . . intimate." Cate ran her hand up his bare arm. "Now what shall we do tomorrow for our first full day here? There are still two spots on the full-day Daintree River cruise, according to the desk."

"A full day on a river?" John repeated.

"It's called a river cruise, but the river is just part of the excursion," Cate explained, using the wet on the outside of her champagne glass to remove the stickiness of her husband's sweat from her hand. "They take you through the Daintree National Park and to Cape Tribulation, too."

"Cape Tribulation. Sounds like there's a story there."

"There's a story everywhere here. Captain Cook ran his ship aground on a coral reef off Cape Tribulation in 1770 and later famously said 'There began all our troubles.'" She pulled a face. "Apparently it took a bit to make the ship seaworthy again."

"Sounds fascinating." John slid an arm around her. "I'm sorry I haven't been a very good sport."

"No worries, I'm simply going to have to show you a good time," she said, slipping away from him playfully. "Shall we go see our room?"

——

"I have to admit our bungalow is super," John said, as they made their way back to the main lodge for dinner. "That double hammock? And the outdoor bathtub, wow."

"I told you it was special," Cate said and held up her hand. "Just stop for a second and listen."

"To what?"

"The rainforest breathing."

The rush of the Daintree River was all he could hear at first, but gradually other sounds emerged. A whoop, whoop, whoop. A low twee, twee. Then a nearly earsplitting awk, awk, awwwk, followed by a throaty chuckle.

"What is that?" John asked, glancing around the dense foliage on either side of the path.

"I have no idea," Cate said. "But isn't it beautiful? Animals, birds, insects we've never heard before. And even familiar ones sound different here."

"And the river is . . ." He was attempting a three-sixty, trying to locate the direction of the sound. "There?"

Cate nodded. "The lodge is set above the river, so there are steps—quite steep steps, from what I remember—on each end of the grounds. One here, by the main building, and another on the far side by the boat landing. We'll hike the river trail tomorrow or maybe the next day if we do the river tour tomorrow." She smiled in the dark and hooked arms with him. "There are crocodiles, though, so we'll have to be careful."

"I'm game," John said heartily, if a tad strained.

Cate laughed. "We'll stop at the desk after dinner to sign up. I'll get you loving this place, one way or the other. You'll never want to leave."

"Let's not get ahead of ourselves. Dinner first, before signing up for life," he said, catching sight of a sign pointing to the lobby and dining room. "Up these stairs?"

"Up these stairs," she said, grasping the rail and leading the way up. "Watch your step."

———

"Yes, the two spots are still available. Shall I sign you up?"

"That would be lovely"—Cate glanced at the young man's name tag—"Noah. And is the tour guide that very colorful man . . . I can't remember his name."

"Leo," Noah said. "And yes, he's still the man."

Cate grinned and turned to John. "You're going to love Leo. He's a real character."

"I'm sure," John said, and turned back to Noah. "And what time is this tour?"

"Leo will get you at nine sharp from the parking lot up front. There'll be," he counted, "six of you on tour, it seems."

"Perfect," Cate said, glancing at John. "Sound all right, darling?"

"Sure," John said.

"You're not just saying that, are you?" Cate asked. "Because if you'd prefer to stay around here tomorrow, I'm fine with that, too."

"There's plenty to do on-site," Noah said, nodding. "We have bikes for your use, and there are miles and miles of walking trails, of course. We only ask that you stop by the desk and let us know where you'll be before you head out. We're happy to pack you a lunch, if you like, as well."

"Do you have kayaks?" John asked. "And can we swim in the river?"

"Now the Mossman Gorge is lovely, and we're happy to run you over in the lodge's ute," Noah said. "There's the Cultural Centre there and swimming and kayaking on the Mossman River at our sister lodge."

"Mossman. That's different from the river we're on?"

"This is the Daintree River just here, sir," the desk man said. "And since there are seventy adult crocodiles that roam the Daintree, we ask that you do not swim or kayak from the lodge property. We'd hate to lose you."

"That tour is sounding better and better," John said, turning to Cate with a smile.

"For the first day, I think." She smiled back at him. "Until we get our bearings, it'll be a nice introduction to the area."

"Until I get my bearings, you mean," John said, with a grateful nod to Noah as they left his desk.

"Ahh, that's what's bothering you," Cate said. "Am I sounding like a know-it-all?"

He turned to face her and took her hands, "No, you're sounding like somebody who has been here before."

"With my mother and father first. And then mourning their deaths," she reminded him. "Not exactly a romantic trip, but I remember thinking as I watched everybody else, that the lodge would be a lovely place for just that."

"Which is why you wanted to come with me," John said, a little shamefaced. "I'm sorry."

"But?"

"But I guess I'd like our next trip to be somewhere entirely new to both of us. Someplace we can discover together."

"Deal," she said. "Unless you'd like to introduce me to Paris. I've never been."

"That is a wonderful idea. I'll show you the things most tourists miss, like . . ." He wagged a finger at her. "Oh, I see what you're doing there."

She grinned. "What say tomorrow, we let Leo show us the sights?"

"What say we do," John agreed, taking her hand.

———

Leo looked up from the open tailgate of his white Volkswagen van to see a familiar figure wander out the front door—well, you couldn't say door, because the truth was the lodge had no doors, the idea being that tourists wanted the true rainforest experience. Which meant they paid extra for the privilege of dealing with bities, knock 'em down rains, stifling humidity, and, today, 35 degrees Celsius.

Well, Leo would be turning up the air today in the vee-dub, and this bunch better not whinge. Including Cate Berger.

"I think you've sold me on this place," John was saying as they approached the back of the van. "Hello, you must be Leo."

"That I am, mate." He slapped a magnetic "Leo's River Cruise" sign on the side of the van, screeching metal against metal to position it, and then held out his hand. "Leo Smith. There are a lot of us Smiths, Jones, Browns, and the like in 'Stralia." He winked at Cate. "Convicts changing their names, you know."

"Then I'll fit right in," John said, shaking hands. "John Jones."

"And do you remember me?" Cate asked. "I'm Cate Berger."

"Sure do. Took the crossing a couple of years back. Terrible what happened there. You have my condolences."

Cate turned to John. "Leo works the cruise ships, as well. He was the first one to arrive that night my parents died. Leo raised the alarm."

"Well, now. You surely were in no shape," he said, patting her hand.

"There have been some happy changes in my life since then," Cate said. "John and I are newlyweds." She flashed the ring.

"Well done, mate," Leo said, slapping the groom on the back.

"Umm, thanks," John said, trying to right himself.

But Leo had moved on to the next arrivals, touching the brim of his hat. "G'day, mates. River Cruise?"

"Ja," the older man said. "I am Jens, and this is my son, Stephan."

"Good to meet you both. I'm Leo, and I'll be showing you the sights here in the world's oldest tropical rainforest. We'll start out in the vee-dub here, driving to Mossman Gorge in the Daintree National Park and Cape Tribulation before stopping for a nice Aussie lunch. After that, the river by boat. And, at the end, I'll give you a fair treat by dropping you here at the lodge's own boat landing when we finish. Sound good?"

"Absolutely," John said.

"Good on you," Leo said, smashing him in the back again. "Now you climb onboard when you're ready. We're waiting for two more, but they should be along . . . yup, here they are right now."

As Leo turned his attention to the new guests, Cate led the way to the van, sliding into the row behind the driver and patting the seat for her husband to come join her.

"I'm Cate," she told Jens and Stephan as they climbed in behind them. "And this is my husband, John."

"You are Americans?" Stephan asked.

"Yes," John said. "And you—"

"German—from Leipzig," Jens said.

A gray-haired man stuck his head in. "No two seats together?"

Stephan raised his hand. "I am happy to sit up front." He smiled at Cate. "Shotgun, I believe you call it in America?"

"Yes, shotgun," she said, as Stephan climbed past her to the front passenger seat.

"I'm so sorry," a young dark-haired woman said, appearing at the van door. "Russell and I don't necessarily have to sit together."

"Oh, but if we do, I can explain the sights," the older man said. "You don't mind, do you?" he asked, sliding in next to Jens.

"Not at all," the German man said. "I'm Jens."

"Pleased to meet you," the woman said, reaching past her companion to shake hands. "I'm Anna."

"Great nails," Cate said, trying not to catch herself on the young woman's red-white-and-blue stiletto manicure as they shook. "Are you American?"

"Canadian," Anna corrected. "Red, white, and blue for the Australian flag. In honor of the trip, you know."

"We're from Toronto," her companion said. "Though I've been here several times, so feel free to ask me anything."

"This is Russell," Anna said, with a trace of apology in her smile. "Once a teacher, always a teacher."

"Is that how I came across last night?" Cate asked John in a low voice.

"Not a bit," he said.

She elbowed him. "Liar."

"Well, folks," Leo said, getting into the driver's seat. "Welcome to our excursion here. If there's something I don't cover that you're curious about, just ask. I don't know the answer, I'll just baffle you with my bullshit."

"Now this guy I like," John said, and then stretched his back. "As long as he doesn't hit me again."

———

First stop was Mossman Gorge. "Didn't Noah at the lodge say you can swim here?" John asked, as they trailed down the sun-dappled path to where the river opened up to a wide pool of clear, rushing water dotted with large flat rocks. "So why do the signs say not to?"

"And yet," Anna said, taking in the dozen or so people who were either sunning on the rocks or wading through the water. "Everybody is."

Cate was trying to gauge the relationship between Anna and Russell. The age difference had to be thirty years, but they were definitely not father and daughter. But maybe not a couple either. "Liability, I bet."

"Right on you," Leo said, joining them. "But you can't legislate against stupid and, truth is, this and the Mossman River are generally too cold and run too fast to have their share of crocs. Least compared to the Daintree River."

"Like Noah said," Cate whispered.

"We won't swim here at the gorge," Leo continued. "But if the weather holds out, you can break out the bathers at Cape Tribulation."

"That will be the Coral Sea there," Russell informed everybody. "Not either river."

"The weather?" Anna was looking at the gathering clouds. "Is it supposed to rain?"

Leo laughed. "It rains most days this time of year—anywhere from spitting to belting down. We just pay it no mind."

He moved to Cate and John by the water's edge. "Are you crossing to Auckland after this? There's a ship out of Cairns on Monday."

"No," John said, with a quick glance toward Cate. "We're flying back to Sydney for a few days before going home."

"That'll be a fair go, too," Leo said, and then raised his voice. "We'd normally head to the boat launch for the river cruise right about now, but the captain I use chucked a sickie this morning and left us high and dry. No worries, though. I hired a boat later this afternoon to take you on the river myself."

He grinned. "But first, I always like a good lunch under my belt, just in case one of the crocs eyes me up for his dinner. Give 'em indigestion."

Anna frowned and raised her hand. "Then we're having lunch now?"

"Nope, ten thirty's a little early even for me," Leo told her. "We'll head up to Cape Tribulation first."

"Goody," John said to Cate as they made their way back to the VW. "And then on to being eaten by crocodiles."

"But not until we've had a good lunch," Cate reminded him.

———

It started to rain about an hour into the ninety-minute drive from Mossman Gorge north to Cape Tribulation.

Cate craned her neck to see out the windshield. "Is Cape Tribulation where we saw that plant that can kill you?" she asked Leo.

"Great." John was playing with her fingers. "Even the plants can kill you."

"Cate is talking about the gympie-gympie," Leo said. "They call it the suicide—"

"Excuse me, but there are emus in the rainforest?" Jens interrupted. "I see a sign."

Leo slammed on the brakes and jammed the van into reverse to back up fifty feet to two stacked amber signs on a pole.

"Sorry, I was yammering and almost missed this," he said. "It's southern cassowaries, not emus, that we have in far north Queensland. You can tell a cassowary by the crest, or casque, on its head and the flashy colors—black body, bright blue neck, and red cape and wattles. Not that you'd have any trouble picking one out. They're nearly as tall as an emu and as mean as they come."

"Large cassowaries can stand nearly two meters; that's more than six feet." Stephan had out his guidebook. "And they weigh seventy-six kilos, or one hundred sixty-seven pounds. Interestingly, this is one species where the female is bigger than the male."

"Mine is bigger than yours, apparently," Cate leaned in to say to John. "There is a circle-of-life feeling up here, isn't there?"

"Can they fly?" Anna asked.

"No ma'am," Leo said, "but they can jump more than two meters straight up in the air and can make their way on both land and water. They've clocked them right here in the rainforest at forty-eight kilometers—or thirty miles—an hour."

"They kick, too." Stephan was reading. "'Their sharp daggerlike claws grow up to four inches long. Can slice and puncture any animal that is a threat, including humans.'"

"About two hundred people are attacked every year, mostly from being careless," Leo said, slipping the van into Park. "If you should come on one, just back away slowly and put something like a tree or a backpack between yourself and the bird. Let it move along."

"So why are we stopping here?" John asked uneasily. "Are we getting out?"

"I think the chance of a cassowary trotting up to us is unlikely," Cate said, putting her hand on the door handle. "But we can look around."

"It's these signs I wanted to point out, and we don't have to get wet to see them," Leo said, turning down the windshield wipers. "The top one is to let drivers know to be careful of cassowaries." The sign showed a black silhouette of a standing cassowary on the amber background.

"Huh. Like a deer-crossing sign in the States," John said.

"Then there's this bottom one," Leo continued, "to warn there's speed bumps ahead." This one was a black half circle, cut side down on a black line, to depict the speed bump.

"But you see what somebody did?" Russell said, standing up to point.

"They've drawn a casque and beak on one side of the speed bump and feet on the other to make it look like a downed cassowary."

"'Before' is written on the top sign and 'after' on the bottom," Jens read. "Oh, yes. I see—that is clever. The cassowary will end up as a speed bump if drivers don't slow down."

"The authorities just leave it that way?" Stephan asked. "That is very cool of them."

"Reckon?" Leo said. "But no, the pollies replace that sign regularly. But soon as they do—"

"It's back this way," Russell took up, delightedly.

Leo put the van into gear. "Maybe it's one person or maybe it's anybody with a marker pitching in. That would be my bet. It's the way things are done around here."

John chuckled as they pulled back onto the road. "Got to love these people."

"Tell them about the microwaves," Russell called up to Leo.

"Oh, yeah," he said, slamming on the brakes again. "There's one right there."

"Where?" John's head was swiveling before he picked it out. "Is that a microwave oven planted on a pole by the street?"

"It surely is," Leo affirmed.

"I don't get it," John said, squinting through the rain. "There's something painted on the door."

"House number or sometimes folks' names," Leo said. "It's a mail bin."

"Male *bean*?" John repeated.

"Mail bin. They repurpose old microwaves as mailboxes," Cate translated. "Keeps the mail dry for pickup or delivery."

"I love this place." John was shaking his head.

"Told you," Cate said.

———

"Last stop before lunch, Cape Tribulation," Leo said, pulling into a gravel parking spot and turning off the ignition. "Sorry about the rain, but feel free to change into your bathers in the toilets here if you want to take a swim."

"No crocodiles, right?" John asked.

"Not probably," Leo said. "But the rest of us can keep watch just in case." He snickered and wandered in the direction of the bathrooms.

"I'm never sure whether he's playing with me or not," John said, as he and Cate waited for the rest of the group to change or otherwise utilize the facilities.

"Sorry, Leo," Cate said as the tour guide returned. "Do I still have time to use the toilet?"

"Long as you make it snappy," he said.

As Cate started up the wooden walkway, she nearly collided with Anna.

"There's no water in the bathroom," the girl told her. "Not even to flush, but if you have to go, I guess . . ." She shrugged.

". . . you have to go." Cate glanced over her shoulder to the trailhead where John and Leo had joined the rest of the group. "Are you and your . . ."

"Friend," Anna supplied. "Russell was my professor, and we found we liked to travel together, if you're wondering. Nothing more."

"I'm sorry," Cate said, casting about for an innocuous reason for the inquiry. "He just . . . well, you both look familiar."

"I used to have blond hair, if that helps, though I can't imagine where we would have run into each other." Anna was searching through her bag and came up with a hairbrush. "But as Russell keeps saying, he comes here a lot. Maybe you saw him with another former student. Hard to tell us apart."

"No, I—" Cate felt her face get warm.

"No worries." Anna touched her arm. "See you down there?"

"Of course," Cate said, turning toward the waterless bathroom.

———

"Beautiful," John sighed, taking in the vast expanse of beach. "Absolutely breathtaking."

"You're standing at the very place that the rainforest touches the Great Barrier Reef," Leo said, nodding across the water. "Wish it were better weather for you folks. But feel free to jump in and swim if you like."

The lowering clouds and drizzle made the prospect less than enticing, and they all just looked at each other.

"Well, if nobody's game," Leo continued, "we'll start up this trail here to Lookout Point. It's a little steep, but here's hoping nobody will stroke out."

"Or the plants get us," Cate said, playfully brushing the back of John's bare leg.

He jumped. "Funny."

"Now, Cate was asking about the gympie-gympie," Leo said, pausing. "If you look right there, about two feet off the path you'll see a shrub with large heart-shaped leaves with serrated edges."

John leaned forward, being careful to stay upright and with his feet solidly on the dirt path. "Looks innocuous enough. Almost fuzzy."

"People say it's the world's most dangerous plant," Cate said, putting her hand on his arm as he leaned in closer to see. "That fuzz is tiny needles that you can't get out."

"Won't kill a person outright," Leo told Cate. "But he'd be in a world of hurt for a couple years, give or take. Wouldn't be able to work, wouldn't be able to do nothing."

"They say it feels like being burnt with hot acid and electrocuted simultaneously," Russell said. "The pain is so bad people have been known to kill themselves, hence the nickname, suicide plant."

"Story is one poor bloke used a couple of leaves as toilet paper," Leo said. "Shot himself."

"Jesus." John backed away, nearly stumbling off the path in the other direction. "Isn't there something they can do for it? To get the stickers out?"

"I've heard adhesive tape or that hot wax works some," Leo said. "You know, put that on and pull it off. Can't get all of them, though, and God knows what it feels like in the process."

John shuddered, centering himself on the path. "Anybody for lunch?"

———

Lunch was at a small open-air café in the bush, and afterward they boarded the VW to drive south to the tour-boat dock.

After pulling into the dock's parking lot, Leo climbed out and yanked his magnetic sign from the side of the van, gesturing for the group to follow him down to the boat.

"That's it?" John asked, surveying the boat's flat floor, tattered canvas roof, three rows of metal benches, and single aluminum rail.

"I believe so," Jens said, passing him to board. "As Leo is applying his tour sign."

In fact, Leo was leaning the sign against the helm. "Probably won't stick," John muttered. "Everything is aluminum."

With a sigh, John followed the German onto the boat. It was still raining on and off, mostly spitting, as Leo had called it, the river a study of greens and grays as they made their way south.

"But bugs," Stephan was saying to Cate. "There were bugs on the lunch menu."

Cate laughed. "They were Balmain bugs, Stephan. Like small lobsters."

"Split 'em open, little oil, salt and pepper, slap 'em on the barbie." From the helm, Leo brought his fingers to his lips. "Mwwah."

"You should have tasted mine, John," Cate told her husband. "You would have loved it."

"I'm allergic to shellfish, remember?" John was at the rail of the riverboat. "And I have to assume that includes bugs."

"You didn't eat much of your barramundi, though," she said. "I'm not quite sure why you asked for a to-go box. You can't really intend to finish it in the bungalow."

"Just being polite." He was peering toward the riverbank. "Holy shit."

"Holy shit what?" she asked, going to join him.

John was leaning on the rail to get a better look. "Is that a crocodile?"

"Where?" Cate asked.

"There, by the shoreline."

"I think it's a tree limb," she said, squinting.

"I believe that the tree limb has opened its mouth." Stephan pointed.

Leo put the boat in idle and came to the rail. "That's Scarface. See?

He has no teeth, but somebody videoed him the other day eating a whole feral pig. And another caught him gumming a cow, but they think the cow was already dead when Scarface found him."

"According to the guidebook," Jens said, coming over with the thing in hand. "Crocodiles have sixty-six teeth and replace them throughout their life, usually with a new tooth every month or two. How is it that this one has none?"

"Like people. They get to be old geezers, and their tooth sockets and jaw bones deteriorate or get damaged," Leo said, going back to the helm to angle the boat for a better look. "We think Scarface is anywhere from seventy to a hundred. He may not be the looker he once was, but he's still popular with the ladies, mating with at least four that we know of, and he returns to every one of them to check out the young when they're born. Tries to eat any that aren't his."

"Charming," Anna said.

"That's the one I was telling you about," Russell told her. "Patrols this strip of the river all the way down past the lodge."

"Along with five or six other crocs," Leo affirmed. "You're getting a fair treat today, like I said. No other tour boats make their way this far."

Anna was watching Scarface, hand over her mouth. "How long is he?"

"About four and a half meters," Leo said. "That's fourteen and a half feet for you Yanks."

"Geez," John said. "Teeth or no, I wouldn't want to meet him on a dark night."

"And that'll be Stubby, up there," Leo called out, pointing upriver.

"Stubby," Jens repeated as a crocodile came straight down the middle of the river toward the boat, tail stroking back and forth. "Because he is short? Yet he must be nearly five meters long, himself."

"Maybe he's lost a leg or something," Cate suggested. "And has a stub."

"Or drinks lager," Stephan contributed.

They all looked at him.

"I believe a stubby is a term for a bottle of beer here?" he said, positioning himself at the rail.

"Right on you, but this stubby is for *stubborn*," Leo said. "Persistent. Stubby'll track his prey for hours and not because he's hungry. Just loves the hunt."

"Do they use just their tails to propel themselves?" John asked as the rain started to fall more heavily.

"Limbs, too. But the tails are more powerful, as you can see. Stubby can kick himself clear out of the water with it if he wants."

Cate put her hand on her husband's back as the wind picked up. "Can you get video as he goes past?"

"Sure." John had his legs braced against the rail and was leaning out to get a better shot. "Just how do crocodiles compare with alligators, Leo? My mother lived in South Florida for a while, and alligators were all over the place. Swimming in canals, sunning in her backyard."

"That's cause alligators are puppy dogs compared to crocs," Leo said. "You might call gators opportunistic. You're there, they're hungry, sure they'll try to make a meal of you.

"A croc, though," Leo continued, as Stubby cruised past not five feet from the boat. "A croc will hunt you down and eat you for the pure fun of it, on the shore or in the water. I've even seen them take somebody right off a boat."

John stepped back, nearly tripping on Cate's foot.

"I'm so sorry, sweetheart," she said, reaching out to help but only succeeding in pushing him further off-balance.

"Steady there." Stepping away from the helm, Leo put a hand out to pull John back to safety. "Sure wouldn't want your husband to go the way of your parents, now, would we, Cate?"

"That's a little cruel, isn't it?" John said, frowning at the tour guide.

Leo just shrugged.

"We're nearly up to the lodge," Cate told John. "If you like, we can take a stroll along the river before dinner."

"If at first you don't succeed," Anna said in a singsong voice. "Try, try again."

Cate frowned. "What do you mean?"

Anna cocked her head, studying the other woman's face closely. "I mean, if practically dangling your rich husband off the boat didn't get him eaten by a crocodile, why not take him for a walk on the slippery river rocks at dusk, the croc's prime feeding time?"

"Just what are you insinuating?" Cate tried to back away but was defeated by the railing.

Leo rubbed the stubble on his chin. "Now, I don't think Anna here is so much insinuating, as saying it straight out."

"Saying what?" Cate's eyes had darkened. "Who are you people?"

"I was a friend of your mother and stepfather," Anna said. "We all were, in fact."

"Friends—"

"That's probably a bit of an overstatement," Russell cut in. "We only knew them for the first four days of the cruise."

"Before they took their lives," Jens said. "Or your mother took her life and your stepfather died in a valiant, if misguided, attempt to save her. Or so was the story we were told."

"It's the truth," Cate said. "Tell them, Leo. You saw me there, sobbing my eyes out."

"Right crocodile tears, I thought at the time," he said, pressing forward himself. "You see, I was there earlier than you thought, having a ciggie. Just tossed it overboard and moved back into the shadow of the lifeboats when I heard you."

Cate raised her chin defiantly. "Heard me what? Failing to prevent my mother from ending her life? Her suffering? If that's what you think I'm guilty of, Leo, I'll admit it."

"That's just it, though," Leo said. "Sounded more to me like she'd lost her nerve, and you were convincing her to jump."

"She was sick," Cate said. "Terminally ill."

"But not dead yet, in the words of the immortal Monty Python," Russell said. "We all sat with your mother and stepfather every lunch and dinner of that cruise. She was enjoying herself."

Anna nodded. "She told me at the pool that very afternoon that she wanted to hang on as long as she could, as long as she wasn't a burden." Her eyes narrowed. "Did you make her feel like a burden, Cate?"

"No, she . . ."

"Your stepfather was a good man," Jens said. "He wished nothing more than to take care of his wife. She was no burden to him."

"But the cost," Anna said, her eyes widening dramatically. "I was appalled."

"The Canadian and German health-care systems are different, I think," Jens said, turning to Cate. "Your mother was a wealthy person, inherited money from her parents. But the illness. It was taking it all, was it not?"

"No . . . yes, but—"

"You must have been relieved when she talked about suicide," Anna said.

"Except, there was your stepfather," Leo said. "What was his name?"

"Bobby," Cate said. "Like he was a ten-year-old. They'd been married less than four years."

"Yet he stood by her," Anna said. "In sickness and in health."

Cate's lips twitched, but she kept quiet.

"Cate is thinking that money will bring people together, too," Anna observed. "And I guess she should know."

"Fair go," Leo said. "And it's true I can't swear exactly what happened to Hallie. Whether she jumped or whether Cate here gave her a tidy shove."

Now Cate went to speak, glancing at John. "That's—"

Leo held up his hand. "But I did see Bobby go over. He was calling for help, leaning over the rail to spot your mother in the water, and you pushed him. That I could swear to."

"Then why didn't you?" she snapped, folding her arms against her chest. "Swear to it, I mean. There was an investigation."

"And it would have been my word against yours," Leo said. "I was a right wuss, I admit that. But I didn't know these folks then. Didn't know what they all knew."

"Putting the facts together," Jens said. "We grew suspicious."

"They're all crazy," Cate said in a low tone to John, taking his arm.

"I bet . . ." Anna was still watching her. "I bet when the dust settled and you were there in your mother's huge house, you couldn't believe how easy it had been. You could do it again, certainly. This time you'd set yourself up for life, because your mother's illness had taken more than you'd imagined, and huge houses demand huge upkeep."

"Don't you hate . . . What do they call it?" Stephan asked. "Pinching pennies?"

"Exactly," Anna said. "But find the right wealthy guy and stage an accident up here? Who would notice? If anything, you'd be a sympathetic figure."

"Even more so than the last time," Leo said. "You sitting there at the lodge in your widow's weeds."

"How long have you and John been married?" Russell asked.

Cate stuck her chin out. "Thirty-four days."

"Counting the days, love?" Leo asked. "Sweet."

"I expect there's an insurance policy," Russell said. "They often stipulate thirty days survivorship to collect."

"That time was helpful to us, though," Jens pointed out. "In order to return here."

Cate turned to John, putting both her hands on his chest. "Don't believe a word of what they've said, darling. I love you."

Anna frowned. "So he's to believe you'd kill your own mother for money, but not him?"

"That . . . My mother was ill," she said. "She made her own decision. And as for her money, it was an inheritance from her family. It would have come to me regardless."

"That's not true," Russell said, holding up a finger. "Your mother made a will in Bobby's favor. After he died, she wanted the remainder to come to you. But that would be up to Bobby. Legally, he could decide to leave your inheritance to his own heirs."

Cate glared at him, and he shrugged. "I taught inheritance law in Canada. People talk to me."

"Just what do you people want?" Cate demanded. "Even if everything you said was right, which it's not," she assured her husband, "what business is it of yours?"

"That's right," John said. "You can't prove any of this."

Cate grasped his arm gratefully.

"Not to a court," Leo said. "But if Cate planned another accident, like our Anna was saying, that would pretty much prove what she did the first time around. At least to us."

They'd been idling down the river, Leo correcting course every little while, and now there was a splash outside the boat.

Cate glanced around uneasily. "Let us off at the lodge. Now."

"How can I do that in good conscience, not knowing if this man is going to survive the night?" Leo said, nodding at John.

"You honestly can't believe Cate would kill me," John said, putting his hand over hers.

"Aren't you wondering that yourself, John?" Anna asked. "Cate found you through a dating service that connects wealthy people. Brought you up here to the rainforest. What is it they say, Leo? Australia is where everything is trying to kill you?"

"True that," Leo admitted. "But Cate didn't even bother with the cassowary because the odds weren't good enough. And the suicide plant? Well, John would linger too long, and she didn't want that."

"And staging his subsequent suicide back home would be tricky," Anna said, wrinkling her nose.

"And he did not eat the Balmain bugs and have an allergic reaction," Stephan said. "Though that would have been a long shot as well."

"John is not that foolish," Jens agreed. "Besides, somebody at the restaurant might have had an epinephrine pen, if the reaction were severe."

"Which," Leo said, slowing the boat, "left the awkward attempt to 'accidentally' knock John into the water with Stubby swimming by."

"And the proposed walk along the river," Anna said. "So romantic, yet with just the two of them, there would be no boatload of witnesses to swear it was all a tragic accident."

"Witnesses can be a double-edged sword," Leo said. "I don't think I have to tell you that, Cate."

"There's the boat launch." Cate pointed, a little frantically. "Let us off there. This instant."

"You do know," Leo said, angling the boat in that direction, "I blocked out the tour every day of your visit and left two spots open, knowing we'd all end up right here eventually."

"You're insane, and I'm going to report you," Cate said, swinging the aluminum gate open as they idled up to the dock. "All of you."

"I don't think so, dear." John's hand was still grasping her arm as she went to step onto the dock. "And for the record, you did pack a surprising number of black clothes for a romantic trip to the tropics."

"Let me go," she demanded, even as Leo reversed the boat.

"Oh, I will," John said as the boat edged away from the dock. "Right . . . about . . . now."

Off-balance, Cate plunged feet-first into the water.

"Who are you?" she screamed, resurfacing. "Why are you doing this?"

"I'm John Robert Jones." He watched dispassionately as she fought to keep her head above water in the space between the dock and the now still boat. "Bobby was my father. Not that you ever bothered to learn anything about the man who married your mother."

"Until it seemed he was going to inherit her fortune," Anna said, leaning down. "Here, Cate. Give me your hand."

"Thank God somebody has sense," Cate said, reaching up. "Ouch, what . . . ?"

"I'm so sorry," Anna said, checking her fingernail. "Did I scratch you?"

"Oh, dear. Blood in the water," Russell said, shaking his head. "Won't that draw crocodiles?"

"Crocs can only smell when their heads are above water," Leo said. "Luckily for Cate, I don't see— Oh, spoke too soon." He pointed. "There's Stubby, chugging on down here. Likes to follow the tour boats, that boy, case something falls over. And I would wager Stephan's parceling out John's leftover barramundi along the way kept him focused."

Cate's head swiveled to see a dark shape coming toward her in the water. "Help me! I swear I'll tell you everything. Sign a confession."

"Now why would we need that, love?" Leo said, as the crocodile came closer. "The rainforest takes care of its own."

"Circle of life," John said, nodding. "Can't you feel it, Cate?"

"It's a fucking crocodile, you moron," Cate screamed, trying to propel herself toward the stony riverbank.

"Crocodiles are as quick on land as they are in water, I believe," Stephan observed, nose in his guidebook as Leo pulled the boat clear of the dock. "Twenty-four to twenty-nine kilometers per hour. That's fifteen to eighteen miles per hour to you, Cate."

But the blond woman was already scrabbling up out of the water.

"Is Stubby going to let her get away?" Anna asked, wrinkling her nose. "Maybe he ate too much barramundi."

"Shouldn't matter." Leo turned to watch. "Have a go at her, you fat mug," he called to the crocodile.

"That did it," Russell observed. "He's on the bank now and—"

"Oops." Leo ducked his head. "Got 'er just three meters onto dry land. I'd have bet money she'd make it five, at least. Motivated."

The group watched as the crocodile chomped down a second time on Cate's already lifeless body.

"Saltwater crocodiles." Stephan looked up from the guidebook. "Stubby is saltwater, correct?"

"All salties in this river," Leo confirmed.

"Then his bite force is three thousand seven hundred pounds per square inch. Greatest of any animal."

"Is . . ." Anna was squinting into the lowering light. "Is Stubby crying?"

"Crocodile tears," Leo confirmed. "Crocs cry when they eat."

"Well, you learn something every day." Russell cocked his head. "Even me."

"You do, don't you?" John raised a hand as Stubby flung Cate's body off the bank and into the black of the river. "Bon voyage, Cate.

"Oh," he said, turning back to the spot where Cate and the crocodile had disappeared. "And you may not have noticed, but I packed a few black things, too. Just in case."

REED FARREL COLEMAN

SHOOT TO THRILL: A TALE FROM GUN CHURCH

His palms were as wet as his dick was hard. The sweat squeezed into the spaces between the grip's crosshatching. That's when he knew. He knew all at once. Everything there was to know. Everything that mattered. ESFT: Every Single Fucking Thing. The beginning to the end, end to the beginning. His whole world, the meaning of life. Most especially beauty and power, how one was the other and the other the same. The Colt Python, forty-eight ounces of beauty and power drawn in royal blue steel. Its six-inch barrel covered by a ventilated rib. In its cast shadow, the face of God.

Music thundered in his brain—Metallica, AC/DC, Motörhead—the blood in his ears pulsing and on fire. It was good to be alive after seventeen years of utter fucking misery and defeat. Seventeen years of taking it, of being the punching bag, the landing pad, the mat, the target, the bullseye, of being the laughed at and not laughed with. He wasn't Jimmy the Joker, but Jimmy the Joke—the punchline with a pulse. The punch-me-in-the-face kid. It had ever been so. Seventeen years of never being able to get out of his own way. Until now, this second, raising up the Python, arm shaking.

As he did, as he slipped his twisted left index finger off the trigger guard toward the trigger, he thought about Leeza, and how in this moment he conflated the Python's beauty with hers. Her eyes blue as the steel. Her body muscular, sleek, and as threatening as the barrel. How it was Leeza who opened his eyes and breathed life into his body and soul. His body, what he had always thought of as God's practical joke. *He was everyone else's amusement, so why leave God out of it? Wasn't it his doing to begin with?* He sometimes thought he heard God's mocking snicker in the chirping of crickets.

Leeza had brought him alive much as Dr. Frankenstein did the monster, although he was more Igor than monster. Leeza, a woman when all the others were still girls. But it wasn't Leeza who had put the revolver in his hand. Leeza gave him life, but Carter McMillian gave him the gun.

Carter Mac, the guy in Brixton High who disdained the football turds and Xbox nerds alike. Carter Mac who ascended to the kingdom of cool via contempt and condescension. Distant and unafraid, James Dean by any other name. James Dean before the Porsche and without the histrionics. Carter Mac, who drove his dead uncle's Harley and wore his motorcycle jacket as a scar, a memorial, and a warning. *Stay the fuck away from me, far away, unless I shine my light on you.* And that's what Carter Mac had done to Jimmy, shine his light.

Oh, how warm that light did feel. Carter spreading his leathery black wing and folding it around Jimmy so tight to make him feel whole and almost human. Almost.

"Jimmy, you're with me now," Carter had said.

You're with me. If Jimmy had had a last will and testament, he would've demanded those words be inscribed on his headstone. No one had ever extended a hand to Jimmy, let alone an invitation and allegiance. That had always been the worst part of his miserable freakin' existence—the loneliness, the isolation—much worse than the ridicule and taunts. He laughed at himself when he used the word freakin' because he was nothing else if not a freak. *More Igor than monster.*

Born with a stub for a left ear, a palsied and atrophied right arm, and a short left leg, James Tyrone Watson was cursed from birth. No, before, at inception. Even his good arm was rotten, good only by comparison to his feeble right. Some babies are constructed from God's spare parts. When it came to Jimmy, it seemed, God had run out of parts or, at the very least, put him together blindfolded.

Afflicted as he was, he might have been able to adjust to the world had his family loved and nurtured him a little bit. It was to laugh, the very concept of a loving family. His mom, the tweaker queen, a former dog food factory worker, had succumbed to her sadness and demons before Jimmy turned five. When she said her Hail Marys, she prayed for the hour of Jimmy's death, not her own. She didn't pray all that much. She couldn't be bothered with prayer, nor could she be bothered getting help for her youngest son. Not when there was the next hit of shabu to score. Still, she was a blue blood compared to Jimmy's old man. The old man, whose term of endearment for Jimmy was BFA—Botched Fucking Abortion.

A drunk, cruel and nasty to the core, who beat his sons for exercise, he reserved his most heartless derision and brutality for Jimmy. "Boys down at the Dew Drop had a pool whether your momma would pop you out or lose her front teeth first. I bet on her teeth, but dammit, you botched fucking abortion, first came you. I lost a C-note on you." It was a familiar refrain followed by bruises.

His brothers, much older than he, had gotten out one way or the other. Bill Jr. escaped into the army before getting blown to pieces by a Taliban RPG in Afghanistan. He was the lucky one. Tommy, the middle brother, sold a bad batch of Ecstasy to the Grinders, the local biker gang. Their club logo featured a man being fed into the mouth of a hand-cranked meat grinder, blood coming out the business end to spell *Grinders*. Though no one dared confirm it, story was they chained Tommy's arms and legs to four Harleys, each driving in different directions. They pulled his limbs from his torso and fed him to the pigs at Mueller's Poultry and Livestock. No one in Brixton doubted the truth of that accounting.

Carter Mac's dead uncle Bronco had been the Grinders' leader until he wiped out on the main road out of Brixton. It was only upon more careful inspection at the hospital that the ER doctor found the entry wound under Uncle Bronco's left scapula.

"He might've survived the crash, though I doubt it. Compound fractures, broken ribs, a collapsed lung, internal bleeding . . ." the doctor told the sheriff, sticking his finger through a dime-sized hole in the back of Bronco's Schott jacket. "But the bullet is probably what killed him."

"Damn biker gangs. If all they killed was each other, I'd buy the ammo. Keep the body in the cooler, will ya, Doc? The county boys'll be by tomorrow to collect him."

That was a year ago, and the case was colder now than the fridge in which Bronco's body had been stored. Nearly as cold as the case of Jimmy's pig-slop brother Tommy. Both the kinds of cases no one in Brixton lost sleep over or protested about outside Town Hall. Both cases were what the sheriff thought of as "Good Riddance" murders. *Two lowlife scumbags down, a thousand more to go.*

As Jimmy's arm steadied, the Python suddenly weightless in his "good" hand, he remembered the day Carter Mac and Leeza found him sitting in the empty stands behind the school, alone. Of course he was alone. They sat down on either side of him. He remembered wincing, thinking he was going to catch a beating from Carter for crimes real or perceived, or for just being. But no, it was the dragon unfurling his welcoming wings.

"Cool jacket," Jimmy'd said, girding for the attack.

"Here, you try it on," Carter Mac said, draping Bronco's scuffed jacket over Jimmy's shoulders.

"It's heavy."

"Gotta be to protect you if you lay your bike down."

Leeza said, "Wow, Jimmy, it looks good on you. Right, Carter?"

Jimmy felt the heat turning his skin red. Leeza was so close to him, he could feel her breath on his neck. "Nah."

"But it does." She stroked his cheek, stared directly at him. "I mean your body's all fucked up, but you do have cool green eyes. They have these little gold and black flecks in them."

After a few minutes, Jimmy slipped out of the jacket, studying the lining like the Shroud of Turin. "Your uncle's blood is still on it where he got shot."

"It's always gonna be there."

"How'd you get it back, Carter? I mean, it's evidence."

Carter shrugged. "Sheriff gave it to my dad. My dad gave it to me, like as a warning of what could happen to me. Like I give a shit about what my dad thinks. Like he gives a shit about what I become."

That's how it started, and when it started there seemed no endpoint. That one day, the universe decided to stop kicking the piss out of him and give him a little love. All Jimmy saw was the pain that lay behind him, not what the future might hold. Pretty easy to understand how a guy like Jimmy tried to enjoy the sunshine while it lasted. How a guy like him didn't want to question good fortune or look ahead for fear the edge of a cliff or quicksand would be the landing spot for his next footfall. He would take what came. What choice did anybody have except to take what came? Thing was, a mutant like Jimmy felt he had even less of a choice.

That was until now, gun in hand. His willful ignorance vanished, and the through line now appeared as clear to him as the mighty winking eye of God. *Gotcha, Jimmy! Gotcha!*

It began with that day in the bleachers behind school. The seduction was slow to begin with, a drip drip drip of attention and affection. A smile and nod from Carter in the hallway for everyone to see. Leeza looping her arm through his left and walking with him down to the cafeteria. Signals to the other kids to find a different target, that Jimmy was off-limits. Of course, there was always the one kid who needed more convincing than a nod and a smile. Rob Pelski was that kid. Carter convinced him by breaking two of his fingers at the middle knuckle. The sound of the snapping and the pain made Pelski puke on himself.

"You go crying to your momma, and the Grinders will hear about it," Carter said when he was done. "But you can tell anyone else who asks, more of the same is waiting for them if they mess with Jimmy."

It accelerated after that. Carter hanging with Jimmy a few nights a week. Sometimes with Leeza, sometimes not. Carter opening up to Jimmy about his shitty homelife. Jimmy doing the same.

"Man, that's fucked up," Carter would say to almost everything Jimmy would tell him.

They shared beers, smoked some dope, laughed.

But it was his time alone with Leeza that thumped his heart and fueled his fantasies. It was chaste at first, Leeza talking about how all the attention she got weighed on her.

"The guys are pigs, and the girls either hate me or want me. You know what Selena Petrovic said to me?"

"What?"

"That sure, I was everybody's wet dream now, but hitting your peak in high school is just sad. Let's see what your tits look like at forty."

At that moment, Jimmy felt more grief than he did for the deaths of either one of his big brothers. He threw his good arm over her shoulders, pressing her face to his chest, letting her tears soak his shirt. That would have been enough for him because when you're the freak, your expectations are subterranean.

The next time they were alone, it wasn't chaste. She kissed him, deeply, undid his pants, and slid her hand onto him. He was hard. Of course he was. That wasn't the surprise.

"My god, Jimmy, you're so fucking big. There's nothing wrong with this part of you." She was breathless, moving her hand slowly up and down. "Nothing wrong at all."

There was no turning back after that.

The next day, after school, Carter took Jimmy up into the wooded hills outside of town.

"You ever shoot, Jim?"

Jimmy laughed. "Me? Nobody would trust me with a gun or a rifle."

"I trust you." That's when Carter took the Python out of his backpack and folded Jimmy's left hand around the grip. He pointed to a fat trunk of a long-felled oak tree about fifteen feet away. "Go ahead, shoot. It's heavy, but you'll get used to it."

The first shot ripped into the dried wood, sending a shower of splinters into the air. The kickback from the Python nearly sent Jimmy sprawling. The second shot missed by a mile.

"No shame in that, Jim. It's a three-fifty-seven. You don't know what the kickback is like for the first shot, so you just shoot. Everyone misses with their second shot because they anticipate the kickback. Don't worry, buddy. You'll get over it."

Carter showed him. He told Jimmy to pick targets for him, and Carter would hit them or come pretty damned close.

After three weeks of going up into the hills, Jimmy had gotten good with the Python. He wasn't as good as Carter, but he was much better than that first time.

Things with Leeza had come along, too.

"God, Jimmy, I love your eyes," she would say before going down on him. "I love your eyes." She taught him how to return the favor. He wasn't sure which he enjoyed more, giving or receiving.

Near the end of the month, Jimmy sensed this was all leading somewhere. He pushed those thoughts out of his head. He couldn't think where, and he didn't want to think about why. He only wanted to bask in Carter's leather-winged warmth and fall into sleep with the taste of Leeza on his lips.

It was a Tuesday in late fall when Carter told Jimmy to hop onto the back of his Harley. Tuesdays were always a shooting day, but Carter drove straight past the dirt road they usually used to get up into the woods. Jimmy shouted as loudly as he could at Carter, asking where they were headed. The noise of the engine and the wind conspired to make the question pointless. Even when Carter rolled the bike through the gates of the abandoned industrial park, stopping at the razor-wired fence of the decommissioned Hardentine Air Force Base, Jimmy was still unsure of what was going on.

Carter said, "We leave the hog here. Follow me."

After climbing through hidden holes in the fences, hopping over short walls, walking through a maze of buildings, they entered an old maintenance hangar. It wasn't a hangar any longer. Wires ran from a door on the opposite side of the cavernous space to temporary light stands. There was also a set of ratty, wooden folding bleachers against the wall behind them. To their left stood two ten-foot-high stacks of old mattresses. Opposite the mattresses, separated by maybe a hundred feet, was a sandbag wall.

"What is this place?" Jimmy asked in fear and wonder.

"Welcome to Gun Church. I'm here to teach you how to pray."

Ten minutes later, they stood across from one another, Jimmy's back to the mattresses, Carter's back to the sandbags. The lights were on now, and the hum of a generator could be heard from behind the hangar walls. They each wore protective gear cobbled together out of discarded Kevlar vests, flak jackets, hockey equipment, beanbags, and foam rubber. Both peered through eye slits in football helmets covered in ceramic plate inserts and olive camo. The least protected parts of their bodies were their gun hands. In Jimmy's hand, the Python. In Carter's, a Glock 19.

"Don't worry, Jim," Carter shouted across to him. "The ammo are sissy loads. Just enough grains of powder to make it real, but not enough to do bad damage."

"But—"

Carter interrupted. "No, buts, Jim. When I say go, raise the Python and fire at me. I'll fire at you. It's simple and you gotta do it."

Jimmy understood there was an implied *or else* in Carter's words. Nauseous as he had ever been, sweat soaking through his underwear, there was no question that he would do what Carter said.

When Carter said go, Jimmy raised and fired. His shot hit the concrete to Carter's right, sparking like a shooting star. The bullet ricocheted into the sandbags. Carter did not fire.

Later, when they had gotten out of their gear, washed off, and dressed, Carter explained.

"You're one of us now. That was your baptism. What the hell else is there to do in this fucked up town to make a person feel alive?"

They'd been back to church many times since, no longer shooting in the woods. There was no going back once you'd been baptized. So said Carter. The third time at church, they were not alone. A few people from Brixton were there. Some Jimmy recognized, like Dougie from the copy store and Pete from the football team. Some he named by their dress or appearance. There was Goth Girl in her black lipstick, piercings, and Doc Martens. Farm Boy in his bib overalls and shitkicker boots. There was Slick in his fancy clothes, and a few others. The only one who mattered, though, was Leeza. They all took turns, donning the gear, facing down one another. Most missed. One or two hit. The last showdown of each evening featured shooters without protective equipment. The idea being to come as close to the other as possible without wounding your opponent. Jimmy had to confess, it was exciting. Afterward, they'd get shit-faced drunk.

The fourth time changed everything. During the last showdown of the evening, Dougie faced off against the dour Goth Girl. That was a thing in church. Names weren't important, just shooting. Just surviving. Dougie almost didn't. Goth Girl's shot sheared off his left earlobe. The blood and screaming were one thing, but what made it real for Jimmy was the glee on Carter's face.

"Relax, Van Gogh," Carter said, pressing a towel to the wound. "The ladies dig scars."

Jimmy didn't know what made him turn away. He would never know, but he did turn. That's when he saw it, the look between Leeza and Carter and Goth Girl. He saw the look and he knew. He knew what was supposed to seem random or accidental was nothing of the sort. That was when he woke up.

Then came his night, the night he was to stand last against another shooter. So, he stood, Python raised, Leeza facing him, fifty feet away. In her hand a Beretta, the Beretta Goth Girl had held when taking off Dougie's earlobe. As he waited to hear the word *go*, he thought about all he'd learned since seeing the look between the three conspirators. Shooting wasn't enough. They needed more. Now they had it—blood. Jimmy was a lot of things. Wholly stupid wasn't one of them. A taste of blood, a bit of an ear wouldn't suffice. He was right.

In the intervening months, there were more wounds, more conspiratorial looks, different conspirators, new members. Jimmy understood what was coming. He wasn't going to let it come. He had spent a lifetime letting it come.

Carter shouted, "Go!"

Everything happened all at once. Jimmy dropped to a knee. Leeza's muzzle flashed. Jimmy turned, fired, muzzle flashing. The thunder of both shots echoed. Leeza's bullet ripped into a sandbag, sand leaking out onto the church floor. Jimmy's bullet hit Carter Mac in the gut, blood leaking out of him onto the church floor. Carter Mac hit the ground, landing in a puddle of his own blood; his hands moot over the hole in his belly. People were screaming, running. Leeza threw her locked-out Beretta at Jimmy.

"One bullet," Jimmy said, smiling at Leeza.

Leeza now running to Carter, the sounds coming out of her feral. She pressed her hands down over Carter's.

"I'm cold," he said, eyes rolling back in his head, lids fluttering.

Jimmy came and stood over them, the Python still in hand.

"What did you do?" she yelled at Jimmy. "What did you do?"

"Do you know what Wagyu beef is, Kobe beef?"

She ignored the warm blood seeping through her fingers. "What?"

"The ranchers who—"

Carter interrupted, his voice weakening, "I'm really cold."

"The ranchers who raise those cows," Jimmy continued, "they pamper them. Give them beer to drink, feed them special food. They brush them and stroke them, play them music. They do everything to take away all anxiety from the cows. A happy cow makes for good meat. They're the happiest fucking cows in the world right until the minute they get slaughtered."

"What?" she repeated, not comprehending. "Why are you talking about cows? You killed Carter."

As if on cue, Carter's chest heaved, red foam formed around his lips, and he went limp.

Jimmy smiled. "You know one thing those ranchers never do?"

"What?" She cocked her head, taking her red-soaked hands off Carter's. "No."

"They never tell the cows what's coming and never put a loaded gun in their hands."

"Cows don't have hands."

"I only have one, but one was all I needed. You both led me to the slaughter, Leeza, but I wasn't going to be slaughtered."

"I'm going to kill you, you—"

"Moo!"

HEATHER GRAHAM

HELLS BELLS

"Hell's bells."

April winced as Conner Marley muttered the exclamation.

They'd been watching the news—and it had been intense. The killer they were calling "the Stickman" had claimed another victim in the Los Angeles area, and just as the newscaster was going into details, the TV had blacked out.

Other people said *damn* or something a bit more guttural or profane, but Conner let out those two words every time something went so much as slightly wrong.

Other than that . . .

Well, they'd met online, and it was a twenty-first-century given that you had to be careful about relationships forged online. But they'd started out with a chat that became a video chat, and after she had carefully weighed time, the online/video relationship had come far enough for them to meet in person. She had plenty of friends who went out with people after an introduction—but that wasn't for her. She'd tried it once, and the guy, who had appeared to be about perfect, had smelled like a dung heap and spat like a trucker and was rude to others to go along with it. No . . . she had learned to be careful.

And Conner was pretty close to perfect. So much so that they'd moved in together after three months of dating. He was an ex-marine, built like a Greek god; tall, gorgeous, with a quick and easy smile. Yes, almost perfect. It was just that the "hell's bells" drove her crazy.

She was nuts to let such a thing bother her so much.

He was amazing to look at, easy to laugh with, an incredible lover—and he had a job, a good one. Employment had been a prerequisite for her, having spent a year of her life right after college supporting a musician who was going to "hit it big" at any time.

"What is it?" she asked, wondering if her impatience could be heard in her voice. He was studying the wires, the cable box, and their entire entertainment system.

He glanced at her, dark eyes somewhat amused, but a frown on his forehead. "This fray in the wire. I think I could get it back on—for now. But it needs to be fixed. I'm afraid we're risking a fire."

"All right. Can you fix it, or do we get someone in here?" she asked.

"I'll have to head to the hardware store," he said. "But, yes, I think I can fix it."

She arched a brow. "Nothing like the CEO of a travel company fixing a faulty wire!" she said, forgetting about *hell's bells*.

Because, of course, he was amazing. He could fix things. He told her that his stint in the Marines had been better than any education at any college ever. But then again, he'd used his time in the Marines to go through college, and thus he was able to hold his job.

She was in love. She thought she was in love, at least. Or, as they said, in love with the idea of being in love. No, Conner was amazing, and, if anything, she was the slacker in the relationship. He was at the top of his game; travel had never seemed more important to people than when they had spent a few years locked in with the pandemic. Meanwhile, she illustrated children's books. She loved what she did—but this time, he was the real breadwinner. Their house, in a pleasant section of San Diego, had largely been acquired with his share of the down payment, and he didn't mind the fact that they shared the ownership of the house.

"So," he said. "Dinner is in the oven. Do I have time—"

"The roast still needs thirty minutes to an hour, even for medium rare," she told him.

"Great. I'll run out and I won't be late. You're an amazing cook."

April laughed. "I'm not an amazing cook. I'm so-so, but my mom taught me that you cook a roast slow . . . keep it tender! Anyway—"

He suddenly pulled her into his arms. "You are an amazing cook. Amazing just to be with. Amazing green eyes, like emeralds, but with the mischief of a cat's eyes! Skeins upon skeins of dark red hair, and your talent!"

Her smile deepened. "I can draw cute little penguins decently."

"I'll try to stop with the *hell's bells*," he said.

She winced. "Sorry! It's just—"

He shook his head. For a minute, his eyes were distant. "It's just something we got used to saying when I was in the service. I don't know who started it. Maybe Sarge Billy; I'm not certain. But it came to be a warning. Something we said when someone spotted something out of the ordinary. It was hell all right, so I guess that *hell's bells* just came into being. Ring those bells in hell when something might go down and go down bad."

"Hey! I'm sorry—it's no big deal," April assured him. "You . . . well, in all honesty, you could complain a whole lot more about me!"

He shook his head, grinning. "I'll be back. Keep the doors locked. I wish we could have heard more about the Stickman before the TV went blank. Stickman!" He closed his eyes, shaking his head. "I've been on the battlefront, and I wonder how anyone can be so sick, killing people with dozens of stabs from a screwdriver. We need a dog."

"We don't *need* a dog. You almost taught me how to shoot, remember?" she asked him. "But I do *like* dogs."

"There is nothing like a good dog," he said. "And I am going to take you back to the range."

She wrinkled her nose. "I don't like guns."

"I don't *like* them either. But they serve a purpose when necessary."

"Would you go get the wire or whatever we need?" April pleaded.

"Do it and come back and then . . . dinner, dessert, coffee, and more dessert, different dessert!" she teased.

"Heading to the front door," he promised.

"Hey!" she called.

"Yeah?"

"When you're back—and maybe manage to fix that thing—"

"Oh, ye of little faith!" Conner protested.

"A comedy!" she teased.

"No sappy rom-com!"

"No . . . um, repeats of *The Big Bang Theory*. Even *Friends*! Just . . . something funny!"

He looked at her strangely and shrugged before saying, "The truth shall set you free."

"Right, but it won't give you very good 'dessert' tonight!"

He laughed as he walked out.

"Watch the news on your phone!" she called to him.

He locked the door as he left. April found herself following him and making sure he had locked the door.

She realized even the snippet of the news they had seen had creeped her out. Conner had been right about one thing—the victims this killer had chosen had died extremely tortured and gruesome deaths.

Los Angeles! City of Angels, home to Hollywood. They were in San Diego. They were far from the craziness that could be LA. She was safe here, and Conner would be right back.

She just wished they had put in an alarm system. It was on their list—and they'd have one soon enough.

She headed into the kitchen, thinking about the house. They had already talked about marriage.

She could have said she was ready—he would have proposed.

But . . .

There had been that thing. That *hell's bells* thing. She needed to get over it. He was truly wonderful. The house was incredible—they had three bedrooms, a great parlor, three baths, a big kitchen with a walk-around island in the center, and a breakfast booth.

The house sat on two acres of land, and they were in a zoning section that would allow them up to two horses if they ever wanted to indulge in riding.

Everything was . . .

Too perfect?

Except for hell's bells!

Whatever. Maybe he'd quit saying it. She dug into her purse, grabbed her phone, and set it to her playlist. With a mix of classic rock and alternative notes, she headed in to check on the roast. It looked as if it was coming along beautifully.

The table was set—she'd opted for using their good plates tonight. When they were both working, there were plenty of nights when they agreed on paper plates, but tonight was Saturday, and while she might work on a few of her sketches for *Papa Penguin's Prizes*, she was working well to meet the deadline, and she could sketch at leisure if she chose.

Mashed potatoes were on warm, and the broccoli was steaming away.

Conner wasn't back.

She could sketch; instead, she took a seat at the kitchen table, picked up her phone, and, despite herself, turned off her music and keyed in the local news.

She shouldn't have done so.

The picture of an attractive blond came to her screen with the caption, "Latest victim of the Stickman killer, Vera Garcia, killed last night between the hours of six and ten p.m."

April wanted to set the phone down.

She didn't. She continued reading. This time, a witness had seen the killer leaving the young woman's apartment building—they had even spoken briefly. A pleasant encounter. The witness had assumed the strange red on the killer's shirt had been part of his costume—the man had explained that he was working on a crime drama series and that he was an actor.

He'd never thought it could be blood. *Real* blood.

But now, the police had a description of the man. And they had an artist's sketch, a rendering of the Stickman as described by the witness.

Tall, about six three.

Well built, as if he exercised regularly.

Dark hair, dark eyes.

Sculpted face. Generous mouth. A man in his early- to midthirties.

April jumped to her feet, dropping her phone. It froze on the artist's rendering of the Stickman killer.

It could have been Conner.

Six three, well built, early thirties, dark eyes, dark hair . . .

No, no, no, no, no.

Polite and charming, the witness had said. Conner was all that. Just as Ted Bundy had been charming, using a ruse to seek help from his intended victims.

No. What was wrong with her? It was one thing to be annoyed by the man saying *hell's bells* all the time, quite another to suspect that he might be a heinous killer!

And then, of course, it had all taken place in Los Angeles and . . .

Conner hadn't gotten home last night until almost eleven, claiming he'd had a meeting with a youth group traveling to Europe the following week.

She was just being crazy. There had been five previous victims, and Conner had certainly been with her when the other women had been killed. But she couldn't remember dates and times exactly; the killer in Los Angeles had been news, of course, a worry, but not . . .

Not something that had frightened her. She lived with an ex-marine, for God's sake!

But now . . .

Dates. Date and times. She needed to look up the dates and times when the other victims had been killed, and she needed to remember if she and Conner had been together or not during those events. And she needed to do it all quickly. Then what? Call the police? Get the hell out and call the police?

She hurried to find her purse again, searching it for the paper calendar she kept, so that she could draw up the times of the murders on her phone and compare them.

But she had barely taken a seat again when she heard the front door open.

"I'm back!" he called. She heard him laugh. "'Here's Johnny!'" he called teasingly, referring to a line from the Steven King thriller *The Shining*.

Stay calm, stay cool, stay collected! April commanded herself. Pretend like nothing's happened, like I haven't seen anything, like . . .

She jumped to her feet as he came into the kitchen. So much for cool and collected. She probably looked just like a mouse cornered by a cat.

She was cornered, of course. She might be a respectable five foot ten, but Conner was indeed a full six foot three and . . .

And as muscled and fit as an ex-marine might be expected to be.

He frowned, looking at her. "Did I scare you? I'm so sorry. I thought I made enough noise coming in."

She had to play it cool. She'd had performance and improv classes in college. Her specialty had been the visual arts, but she had a fine arts major and had enjoyed dabbling in theater, dance, and music as well.

She could do this!

She forced a smile.

"Just in time. The roast is ready to come out."

"Need help?"

"No, no. I've got it!" she said. She turned, grabbed the oven mitts, and headed over to the stove. In a minute, she had the roast out.

She could throw it at him. The roast was hot and the juices could boil his face, blind him . . .

And if she missed . . .

He'd grab, bind her, and start stabbing her over and over again with a screwdriver, or scald her first and maybe . . .

She set the roast down on the breadboard on the island.

"Want me to carve?" he asked.

"No, uh, mind getting the salad out of the refrigerator? And you can grab a plate for the broccoli."

"Got it!" he assured her.

He was working close to her. She flashed a smile his way. For a moment, she wondered what was wrong with her. This was Conner. They laughed together, dreamed together, slept together, and she loved him . . .

BTK's family had not known about him for years. Ted Bundy had fooled every coworker. Some people could wear two faces and wear them so convincingly that . . .

"Oh, hey, this is all set," Conner said. He pulled her close suddenly, kissing her briefly on the lips. "I'll get that wire in. It will only take a second. I'll be done before the roast is on the table!"

That was it. She could slip out the back door. She could run.

Run where? Their property was a good size. What if a neighbor wasn't home?

The car. She had to get to the car. But she had to be subtle and cool about it. Dinner first; fun, fine, and casual.

She finished getting the food to the table. As promised, Conner managed to redo the wiring on the television.

"News for dinner? I thought we were going with a comedy!" she said, as, once again, the news flashed onto the screen.

"Right. Just one second. I want to see what they have on this guy," Conner told her.

He wanted to see what they had on the guy. Dear God, he would see the artist's image, he would see himself. And he would see that she saw . . .

"No! Comedy. You promised," April said.

He came to her. It took all her effort not to bolt, not to scream. Standing in front of her, he drew his knuckles gently down her cheek. "April, we need to know about this guy. Know how he's getting his victims. I know he's been striking in Los Angeles, two hours away, but that's too close. I love you. I need you to be aware and alert and . . . I can't lose you."

His words . . . they sounded so real. She felt herself melting into him, feeling the strength and power of his arms.

"Let's fix our plates, bring them out to the living room," he said.

He began to do so, not waiting for her agreement.

"This killer has struck in many ways."

The words were spoken by a representative from the police

department. He continued for all the different media types at the news conference:

"Missy Granger was taken from the parking lot of a west side mall; Belinda Montgomery was attacked in her own apartment with no sign of forced entry. They believe that he'd been in her house for almost twenty-four hours, watching her, waiting to make sure that her brother, a houseguest home on leave from the military, was gone. Our latest victim was attacked in her garage. Tara Nelson was attacked after saying goodbye to friends after a night out on the town. Extreme caution should be practiced at all times.

"Again, we have an artist's rendering of the witness's description of the man seen leaving the last crime scene. Our best advice is to stay in groups as much as possible. Be vigilant when it comes to locking doors. Anyone with any information regarding this killer is urged to call our hotline. Every officer in the city and state is actively involved in this investigation. Please, be wary, be vigilant."

The artist's rendering flashed onto the screen.

"Oh, my god! That could be me!" Conner said.

April forced herself to be calm and nonchalant.

"Oh, Conner! That could be any guy. There are only so many face shapes and ways an artist—with someone just describing someone—can make a man look. That could be anyone."

He shook his head. "I wonder if I should head into a local precinct and tell the cops that I didn't do it. I don't know. I think it looks like me. And I'm insulted." He tried to smile. "I thought I was more unique than that."

"You are unique!" April said, and she was surprised by the passion in her voice. Was it possible to be this conflicted? This terrified of a person—and equally determined that it couldn't be?

He shook his head, staring at the television screen. "This is . . . wow."

"And you know what? I said comedy. This guy strikes in Los Angeles. As you said, we're at least two hours away, depending on traffic. That's his comfort zone. Could we please have dinner and watch some reruns of a sitcom, please?"

He nodded, but he still looked troubled.

As she was herself. She was the one who needed to get to the precinct!

She walked to the TV table, found the remote, switched to a streamer station, and found the latest season of a beloved comedy show.

"There. Now, we need to enjoy the roast beef!"

He nodded, and they sat in silence until a line in the show made them both laugh and then glance at each other and smile.

"Hey," April said quietly. "A sun flare could blow up the planet at any time. A whacked-out dictator could hit the button on a nuclear weapon. There's always bad around us, but—"

"I can't control the sun," he told her. "Or crazy dictators. Also, I think I saw him once—"

"You saw him?"

"I've got to get to the police. Tell them what I do know. I can only worry about the things that I can control. I have to go to the cops. They have to have something that can prove my innocence. They never give away what they have, but they must have fingerprints, DNA, something."

She nodded.

"Okay."

What would she do when he left? Would he really go to the police? If they had fingerprints or DNA, wouldn't they have traced it to someone already?

Was it all a ruse, and would he come back, and that night, when she lay curled against him, would he pull out a screwdriver and slam it into her heart and her face and . . .

"All right. I understand," she said.

"Let's pick up first!" he said. He seemed happier; he was in control. He'd made a decision. And he was ready to move.

"I've got the dishes. No big deal," she told him. "Go!"

He nodded again and headed out the front. "The door!" he called to her. "April, lock the door. It's incredibly important that you do so!"

She followed him, double-checking that the door was locked.

She looked around, trying to concentrate on the mundane to clear her head. Dinner. They'd actually eaten it—roast, broccoli, and pota-toes, all mostly gone.

She needed to get out. Now, while he was gone.

And what if he was innocent? Really heading to a police station to prove his innocence, distraught by the image that so resembled him?

Did love mean faith? But did facts and intelligence—and basic survival instinct—outweigh love?

As the thoughts tore through her mind, she cleaned up after their dinner. Then she made the decision. She had to get out of the house. Get away. She'd think of something. Her sister was up in the Bay Area. She'd tell him that Jennie had called and was in trouble and needed her help.

Decisions were great. Once determined, April looked around for her purse, checked that she had her phone, and walked out to the car—pausing first to make sure she'd locked the back door. The back door was kept locked almost all the time, unless they were having friends over, or just out to play in the pool.

Yes, it was always locked. Wasn't it?

Groaning to herself, she headed back in, walked through the house to the kitchen again, and checked the back door.

Good thing she had. Somehow, they had left it unlocked. Maybe they'd been careless coming in from the pool the day before.

She locked it and headed back out. Leaving the house was definitely the right thing to do now. But . . .

They had both been there all night. Then Conner had been gone for almost two hours. If someone had been in the house . . .

She remembered the news conference. In one instance, the killer had been in the house an entire day.

Los Angeles. They were in San Diego. Far away. Well, several hours away, at the least.

She headed to the car. Keyless entry and ignition, but her keys were in her purse.

The car wouldn't start.

Letting out an "Argh!" of aggravation, April dug into her purse.

No.

Her keys weren't there!

She always kept her keys in her purse. She never had to take them out, unless, of course, Conner was borrowing her car, which he never did—he had a shiny new Lexus. Before he'd gotten the new car, though, his old one had given him fits and he had taken her Rogue.

But . . .

All right. Where were her keys?

Had they fallen out in the living room?

April let out another sound of aggravation. Nothing to do but go back into the house and find her keys. Conner's car remained gone. And it was really ridiculous to think that in a place as large as Southern California, a whacked-out serial killer working in the LA area might be in her house. Unless, of course, the killer was Conner . . .

What if it was Conner? What if his car was just beyond eyesight and he had doubled back on foot, snuck back in the through the kitchen, slipped by her into the bedroom so that he could take her keys, assuring that she didn't leave. What if he had seen himself in the image on the screen and been horrified—not because he looked *like a serial killer but because he* was *a serial killer and might soon be caught?*

No. And she had to quit being such a ridiculous coward. Maybe, even while loving Conner, she was smart to spend some time away. Call Jennie and let her know she was coming up for a few days. All she needed for her work was her computer. And as sisters, they'd always been close—Jennie kept a toiletry bag here just as she kept one at Jennie's.

Maybe she should even tell Conner the truth. But if he was innocent? Did you ever forgive a loved one for believing you might be a heinous killer?

Act like a normal human being, quit being such a ridiculous coward.

She left the car and hurried back into the house, opening the door, wishing they had made putting in an alarm a number-one priority when they'd gotten the house.

Well, they hadn't. And if a killer was in the house already . . .

Ridiculous!

April headed into the bedroom, looking on top of the dressing table where she usually dropped her purse. No keys.

She dropped to the floor, looking over the expanse of the carpet, crawling to look under the bed.

It was then that she heard the front door open and close.

Conner? Was Conner back already?

She didn't have time to ponder the question because she knew immediately that it was Conner, and that he was warning her about something. Because he shouted out, as if irritated.

"Hell's bells, oh, hell's bells!"

A door slammed from somewhere in the house. And then . . .

The door to the room April shared with Conner, where she lay now on the floor, slammed shut as well.

"Bloody bastard!" someone muttered.

"Hell's bells! I do mean hell's bells!"

It was Conner, calling from the front of the house. He knew. How did he know? He'd come back because he knew that the killer was coming . . . to their house in San Diego? Or . . .

April crept the rest of the way beneath the bed.

She barely dared to breathe.

The killer was speaking to himself then, muttering, swearing.

"No, no, no. He's back. He shouldn't be back. Where the hell is she?"

The killer was with her. In the bedroom. Conner was locked out. Conner kept his old service weapon in here, in a lockbox by the bed. Okay . . .

She didn't like guns. But she'd give her eyeteeth for that gun right now. She didn't know if she could hit anything, but . . .

Don't breathe, don't move, don't make a sound! She warned herself.

"Hell's bells, hell's bells, hell's bells getting close, closer . . ."

The door to the room opened. Conner looked in.

April realized the killer had to be in the closet, hiding from Conner just as she was hiding from the killer.

"April?" Conner said.

She didn't dare answer.

A mistake!

He must have determined that she had gone outside because he started to walk away.

No!

She tried to call out. She barely made a choking sound. Her voice seemed to have frozen in her throat.

Then, she felt it.

A grip. A handgrip on her ankle, and then . . . another grip on her other ankle.

Her throat unfroze, and she let out a scream that was loud enough to wake the dead.

Conner was instantly back in the room, throwing himself at the man who had the grip on April's ankles. The killer was quick, responding with a feint that sent Conner flying down onto the bed. And while Conner regrouped, the killer produced his screwdriver.

He tried to strike. Conner dodged.

April stared in horror. And then she realized that Conner was fighting for her life.

And she was doing nothing.

Somehow, she found something within her that resembled courage.

Conner was a formidable opponent, but so was this man. Six three, as Conner was six three. Well-muscled, toned, strong.

The killer had a weapon.

Conner had none.

April had been dragged out from beneath the bed; she had been left slumped against the bedside table.

The killer suddenly turned to her, screwdriver held high. She saw it falling toward her and rolled just as Conner caught the man from behind.

The screwdriver caught Conner in the arm. He shouted briefly in pain.

Blood seemed to fly.

She was such a coward. So pathetic. And she couldn't be. She had doubted him. He was fighting for his life . . . because he'd been fighting for hers.

The lockbox!

She finally found the courage needed and leapt to her feet. Of course, she knew the combination. Conner had always trusted her completely.

Trusted her completely, while she had suspected . . .

78234

She keyed in the number. The door to the lockbox sprang open. His Glock 19 was there, always loaded, always kept in the lockbox.

She reached for the weapon and drew it out, trying to remember everything Conner had ever told her about shooting the gun.

"More than anything," he had said once, grinning and shrugging, "point and aim. Point well and aim true."

She might hit Conner.

No. She could prevent it. He and the killer were locked in a heated wrestling match at the moment, but she had to get them parted.

It was her turn. Her turn to voice the warning.

"Hell's bells, hell's bells, hell's bells!" she cried.

And it worked. Conner disengaged himself, pretending to be staggered by a blow, stepping back.

There was a brief second in which April could study the killer. He was Conner's size, shape, weight, yes. But . . .

He had light shaggy hair; his face was broader, his chin more pointed. The artist's image did resemble Conner more than . . .

He was moving. April had one chance.

"Stop! I'll shoot."

He didn't stop. He seemed to know she was a coward who had never shot anyone.

But this man was heading toward her; he was a split second away, with a screwdriver raised to slam down upon her, straight into her heart from the angle . . .

"Hell's bells!" Conner shouted, seeing all that she saw.

And she did it.

She aimed.

And she fired.

He went down, but so close that the screwdriver in his hand scraped against her body as he fell at her feet. She'd caught him dead in the chest.

In the heart, she thought. And he'd died instantly . . .

And . . .

"April!" Conner stepped heedlessly over the body and enveloped her in his arms.

Shaking, she let him hold her. Otherwise, she'd have fallen.

She heard sirens.

"How?" she whispered.

"The police followed me. I'll explain, but now . . ."

He lifted her, and they stepped around the body. Soon, police were pouring into the room, and she and Conner described the action that had taken place.

There was so much paperwork.

There was a trip to the station. There were media personnel everywhere.

But finally . . .

She showered. She had a few scratches, but she was fine. Conner had a bandaged arm. But they were together and alone—in a hotel room. April hadn't been able to go back to the house that night.

She had to admit the truth.

Cradled in his arms, she looked up at him and said, "I thought it was you!"

And to her surprise, he smiled. "You'd not have been the bright and beautiful woman I love if you hadn't been afraid."

"But you went to the police—"

"I knew I was nowhere near that apartment building. And I thought about a man that I had seen—in Los Angeles—who looked like me. And the supposed 'witness' described someone who looked like me. So, I suspected that the 'witness' just might be the killer—but assumed he was still in Los Angeles."

"What?" she demanded incredulously. "Why would the witness describe someone who looked like himself?"

He shook his head and told her, obviously distressed, "April, it was all my fault."

"But how?" she asked, completely lost.

"I didn't just see him. I talked to him. Actually . . . we've seen him before."

"What? Where? I don't remember ever seeing him," April said, baffled.

"When we went to see my cousin's play in Los Angeles. You went to the ladies' room. I was waiting for you. He came up to me and said that I must be his brother from another mother, and we laughed and talked a minute. I told him that I was in travel, and he said that he had to come see me and . . ."

"And?" April asked.

"I gave him one of my cards. He walked away right when you came back out from the ladies' room, but now I believe that even though you might not have seen him, he must have seen you and . . . Los Angeles is two hours but he stakes out his victims, he . . . oh, April! I never should have left the house. I never should have left you alone. But we were here and . . . April, forgive me, I give my cards out all the time and I didn't think . . . I didn't think! I had no idea that he might be in here, in our house, already!"

"You were right?" she whispered.

He nodded. "Well, I was proven to be correct. A wily detective at the force thought that we should be protected until they could make sense of it all, so an officer followed me back, finally realized what was going on inside, but . . . April, how can you ever forgive me? I swear—I will never put our address on my cards again and, in fact, they'll have an email address on them and that's it!"

"I don't need to forgive you. We all go through life, interacting with others we may not know, just for a minute. And I hope that this doesn't change us, that we still expect the good out of people. No. I need you to forgive me. I was such a coward. I love you, I just . . ."

"Like I said, only an idiot wouldn't have worried. The important thing is . . . don't call yourself a coward. Bravery isn't strutting around like a superhero every day, April. We're all afraid. Bravery and courage are acting—even when we're terrified. And, well, I'm hoping you'll have the courage, too, to become my wife and raise kids with me. Now, that's a challenge these days! Kind of makes me tremble, but, hey, please, I'd get down on my knees but I'd have to let you go. Anyway, let's do this thing. Will you marry me?"

She laughed, and smiled at him. He was perfect. A man who even understood doubt and fear, forgave and loved her.

"You know, this is a strange moment for a proposal."

"Yeah, it should have been with flowers and romance and a candlelit dinner and . . ."

"No, no, I'm not that picky! I mean, it's just . . . it's just . . ." She hesitated and then laughed. "Perfect!" she whispered at last.

"Well?" he pressed softly. "Does that mean . . ."

She curled into his arms.

"Hell's bells! Yes!" she assured him. "Oh, hell's bells, hell's bells, hell's bells!"

CHARLES TODD

HAVE A DRINK ON ME

Sergeants were a short-lived commodity in the trenches on the western front during the Great War. First over the top, leading the rest of the men, whistles blaring, waving everyone to come with him to face the barbed wire, pockmarked shell craters filled with mud and water and bullets. They did not last from wounds and death.

Rutledge only nodded when Corporal Hamish told him the company beside theirs had a new sergeant just reporting for duty. Hamish himself was doing the work of a sergeant since theirs had been killed months ago.

"He's tellin' em he'll na git hit like te others," Hamish told Rutledge.

"He is dreaming of getting a Blighty ticket home."

Hamish nodded his assent and went down along the line checking on the troops.

The only reason they go over the top into No man's land was to get out of the mud, slop, and rats in the trenches, Rutledge thought as he returned to his reports.

It was almost a week later when Rutledge went over to speak with Captain Murray, the commander of the company where the new sergeant was assigned, that he met the man. He was a square of a man, who saluted Rutledge as he passed by. Rutledge paused and spoke to him.

"We don't salute much in here, Sergeant. There is no room, and with all this mud you can barely make out rank."

"That may be true, sir. First time ranks a salute from me," he said with a huge grin. "Sergeant Sullivan, at your service, sir."

Rutledge looked the man over, and *square* was the only word that came to mind. He was as broad as he was tall and there was no fat on him. His big meaty hands would make Rutledge's disappear if they were to shake. Sullivan was wearing three stripes topped with a crown, a color sergeant. This rank was for experienced infantrymen, and from color sergeant the man was well on his way to sergeant major.

"Regular army, I take it?" Rutledge asked him.

"Yes, sir. Proud of my fifteen years. Signed up right at the end o' the Second Boer War, I did."

"Well, Sergeant, keep after them."

It was ten days later when Rutledge got to see the sergeant at work. The word had gone out that they were going over the top at dawn the next day. Rutledge and Hamish were moving up and down their section of line talking to the men, steadying their nerves, and checking their gear. Often, they would move out under full pack expecting to take and hold ground. This was a different mission. The sappers had dug under the barbwire in front of the German forward trenches as well as one right up to their defenses. The plan was to blow the mines right as the men went over the top and rushed the German line. If they took the front trench line that was a bonus. Often the Boche would rush the front trenches from the secondary line of trenches. In which case they would grab any papers and prisoners they could and race back to their own lines.

As Rutledge neared the next company, he could hear Sergeant Sullivan doing the same with his men.

"Remember, lads, you'll have a drink on me at The Devil's Tavern on the two-year anniversary o' the peace. Whiskey, gin, and brandy—makes no matter! So join me for a drink, boys. We're gonna make a big noise," the sergeant said to each group of men he spoke to.

It was quite a boast for the sergeant to make. How he planned to make good on his promise was another matter. Rutledge remembered The Devil's Tavern from his days walking a beat in London. The real name of the place was The Prospect of Whitby, and it stood on that spot in Wapping dated from about 1520. The flagstone floor of the place was probably original. The famous London diarist Samuel Pepys used to drink there in the seventeenth century, though by then a new pub had been built on top of it. Back then, smugglers, pirates, and other unsavory types—not to mention its use for cockfighting and bare-knuckle fighting—gave it a hellish reputation and the nickname "The Devil's Tavern." By his time, Rutledge knew it as a bit more wholesome place, but it was on his watch, and he had been called there for a brawl or two.

The men were in their places before the dawn light began to peek over the barren landscape. Silent and ready, a few were saying a final prayer. Letters had already been taken to the rear for the censors and then the mail. It was still and quiet there in the darkness. Did the Germans know they were coming? Had the mines been found? No time to wonder; time to find out. Rutledge looked at his army-issue watch with the glowing hands. He got his whistle out and ready as the seconds ticked by. And then it was time. The last thing before the whistles blew, he heard the sergeant say to his men, "The Devil's Tavern, have a drink on me."

Over the top they went, hunched and running as fast as the barbwire and shell holes allowed. The ground shook as the mines were blown. The Germans were awake now if not before, and sporadic gunfire rang out from their trenches. Then came the machine guns with their withering fire sweeping the field. The Germans kept their machine guns low to the ground. It was the legs they were after. Cut the men down and then kill the men helping the wounded man back to their lines. The bastards that they were. Rutledge was blowing his whistle and pushing the men to make their way to the rim of the exploded mines. Never go in the hole, go around, he had taught his men. The smoke and gunfire were blinding as they tried to keep their direction. No time to stop for the wounded and the dead. They would get what they could on the way back. Rutledge and a few of his men made it to the German trench.

Right as Rutledge was about to jump in, he looked over and saw Sergeant Sullivan yelling and waving his men forward to the trench. He did not look wounded and was standing atop the trench edge encouraging his men to follow before he too leapt into the trench and out of sight from his men.

Resistance by the Boche was determined, and Rutledge found himself in hand-to-hand combat, striking and killing several German soldiers before making his way to a dugout. Inside, he found what appeared to be a mess with tables and a few camp chairs. In a side area dug into the earth was an area that looked to be an officer's quarters. Quickly, Rutledge grabbed all the papers he could see and shoved them into his tunic, then made his way back to the trench where he found Sergeant Sullivan had a German soldier by the scruff of the neck, who looked more like a child than a man.

As he bound the boy's hands, he looked up at Rutledge and grinned. "Captain, hars a young un fer ya. They talk easier." He shoved the lad toward Rutledge, turned around, and punched a German soldier in the face that was sneaking up behind him. The soldier fell back against the side of the trench and sank to the ground. "Are we done, sir?"

"Yes, Sergeant, let's head back."

Sullivan stepped toward his men. "Come on boys. You will have a drink on me, so let's be off then," he said and began herding his men toward their own lines.

Rutledge grabbed the boy and heaved him up out of the trench into No man's land. Coming up behind the boy, he could see Hamish guiding the men back to where they came. The machine guns were picking up again. Rutledge was sure they had taken out the gun nests in his area of the line. No time to wonder, he shoved the boy in front of him, ducked, and ran behind him. His part of the plan was to get this prisoner to Intelligence and that meant alive.

Tired and soaking wet, Rutledge returned to the hole dug into the dirt, which they called the Commanding Officer's Quarters. Thank God for the bureaucrats at HQ. Rutledge was not sure whether it was an attempt at euphemisms or plain ignorance that came up with the terms used by the commanders. Rutledge tried his best to scrape off the mud that clung to every strand of his uniform and body, but it was a lost cause.

"Sir?" came Hamish's voice from the "door" that was just an army blanket on twine.

"Be right with you, Corporal."

Rutledge opened the blanket wearing the least muddy uniform he could find. Often the troops would sling them over the top to dry and then try to shake the dried mud from the cloth.

"What have you got, Hamish?"

"Yon Germans is na pleased wi our visit. Bringing up five nines, they are."

Five nines were the German 15 cm sFH 13. Called five nines by the men, the barrel was five point nine inches in diameter. They were German heavy field howitzers, and they could tear up an enforced trench and make a terrible mess.

"Have they ranged them yet?"

"Nay, but it won't be vera long afore they do."

Rutledge nodded at Hamish and made his way out of the dugout to the main trench. There was no artillery barrage, not even a shot being fired. Funny the uncanny senses of the men who sat listening to the sounds across No man's land. The joke was they could tell when Fritz had a head cold. Someone had heard them rolling the artillery in place.

Rutledge looked toward the area where Sergeant Sullivan was moving among his men. "Steady now, lads, those square heads are no happy wi our visit today. Don't let them scare ya wi those five nines. Great gun, too bad they don't know how to use it! Remember the drinks at The Devil's Tavern."

Rutledge made his way through the muck and ghoulish mess over to the sergeant.

"Sullivan, a word, if you please."

The man made his way over to him and replied, "Yes, sir. What can I do for ya?"

Speaking quietly, Rutledge said, "You are a good leader of your men. You motivate them and urge them on. I saw that today. You keep talking about drinks at The Devil's Tavern. Is that The Prospect of Whitby in London by chance?"

The sergeant looked quizzically at Rutledge as if he were a stranger. "An how do ya know about the Prospect then? Not a place I would think a gentleman like yourself would be."

"I was a policeman before the war; I earned my way up the ranks. I know more about it than most."

Sullivan looked at Rutledge squinting in the darkness. "Never figured you was a bluebottle."

Rutledge smiled in spite of himself. "You don't sound cockney enough to use that old term."

"I was no born within hearin' distance of the church bells of St Mary-le-Bow, but sergeants meet all types."

"You tell your men that the drinks are on you at The Devil's Tavern two years after the peace. What if something happens to you?"

"No bother, Captain, I will make it through this mess and bring me lads wi me. I know I will be there. They will be there too, just you wait and see!"

"We all could die tomorrow, Sergeant. How many men will show up only to find you are gone and they cannot have a drink on you?"

"Tell ya what, Captain, if ya make it through this mess, come to The Devil's Tavern two years after this is over. It will be a night to remember."

"I may just take you up on that . . ."

Just then the five nines opened up and the ranging began. Ducking and running toward their men, the conversation was over.

The horror of these howitzers was the way they exploded in a trench. All the sandbags focused the charge along the trench. The shockwave came first, followed by smoke, and then the shrapnel from everything in its path. One shell could wipe out one hundred yards of trench. They did not kill; they tore men apart and sent the pieces—along with the mud and everything—flying everywhere.

It lasted all night and into the dawn. Those demonic barrels of death belching the sparks and flames from their gaping throat. The Boche filled their hunger, again and again. They roared, sending their death whistling down upon the land, throwing everything a hundred feet or so into the air only to pause and then fall back. Rutledge and Hamish kept watch over the men in the trenches all night.

At one point, Hamish yelled, "Ware!" and shoved Rutledge into a dugout. Hamish fell in behind him, and a shell came in seconds later, landing close to their previous position.

It continued sporadically all day and into the next night. The only hope was the Boche would move the guns to another place in the line. Until then, the unrelenting hell would continue.

Rutledge dodged his way over to Captain Murray's area, and they discussed the raid the day before.

"How did your men make out yesterday?" asked Rutledge.

"As well as can be expected. More young men not going home again," Murray replied. Murray was a good officer who genuinely cared about his men. Like Rutledge, he was not regular army. Before the war, Murray had worked installing and designing fire suppression systems in Manchester. His was a world of pumps and waterlines that would douse fires in the mills and warehouses. He was used to recruiting his crew of men in peacetime, not commanding them in war and death.

"I assume we will never know if we got anything important for the intelligence officers," Rutledge replied.

"You and I know better than to expect anything that would tell us what was going on. That is for the higher-ups who need to know the 'Big Picture,'" Murray replied with a laugh.

"True enough," Rutledge replied. "It never gets easier writing those damn letters for the family. King and Country are little solace for their wives and families."

"They did not teach us that skill when we were trained, did they?"

Just then Sullivan came up to the two officers.

"Well, how are you faring, Sergeant?" Rutledge asked.

"Another splendid day at the front, sir," he replied, a bit of sarcasm in his tone.

Turning to Murray, Rutledge asked, "Any word on some artillery to push their five nines back? We are taking one hell of a beating out there."

It was obvious even in the dugout with the hammering from above and the dust falling all around that they needed some relief.

"I am not counting on help anytime soon. You and I know better," Murray replied.

As Rutledge made his way down the trench toward his men, he saw an all too familiar sight. The bombardment had loosened the sandbags and planks that shored up the sides of the trenches. Rats scurried everywhere—not an uncommon sight—and the skeletons of the dead men who had been shoved into the sides of the trenches and planked over caused the men to shudder. Staring up with holes for eyes, their flesh picked clean by the rats, they grinned at the men who uncovered them.

Sergeant Sullivan went down the line, "Steady, lads. Let us send 'em back to the rear and let 'em hav a Christian burial."

Rutledge shook his head and headed for his dugout. Along the way, he came upon Hamish doing much the same as Sullivan. The trenches were in a very bad state, requiring a lot of work.

Looking up as Rutledge approached, Hamish said, "Te damn Boche! Clean it up an tey tear it up again."

"Steady on, Corporal. You know it comes with the glory and ribbons," Rutledge replied.

Hamish grinned and nodded. With a sigh, he turned to the men and hefted a fallen timber.

Rutledge turned and entered the dugout. It was time to do the job he liked the least. At his desk, he stared at the envelopes of personal effects Hamish had gathered from the dead. Now it fell to Rutledge to write to the family. He always made a point to mention something about the men that were lost.

Dear Mr. and Mrs. Moody:

It is with a heavy heart I must write to inform you about the death of Private Harry Moody. Harry was a good lad and well-liked by the men he served with. He often spoke of your flower gardens, Mrs. Moody. He loved the color the flowers brought to the yard and the wonderful scent they added to the wind. He was proud to be the son of a farmer and loved the countryside in Kent. He was quick to remind everyone that Kent was the garden of England.

Private Moody was a brave soldier and fought hard for his country and King. His loss will be deeply felt by myself and the men he served with.

With my personal sympathies,
Captain Ian Rutledge

Signing his name, Rutledge sighed and turned the page to begin the next letter. In all, he had fifteen to write. He knew his letters would be kept and cherished, along with the personal effects, in someone's home. He felt embarrassed that he could not say more about what they were doing and why they died. Of course, if he did, the censors would send his letters back to be rewritten. They did not like to put black censor's marks on letters home from commanding officers who were supposed to "know better."

Finishing his last letter, Rutledge stood up and stretched. He noticed the five nines were no longer being hurled at them by the Boche. Carefully, he made his way out of the dugout and into the trench. Hamish and the men had done the best they could returning the trench walls back to some semblance of order, but *order* was not a word he would use to describe the trench. Walking ankle-deep in the water and muck, he tried hard not to trip over something hidden in the mess. Falling in this would render a man into a mud-caked being, and there was no way to clean it off.

Coming up next to Hamish, Rutledge asked, "How are things settling now they stopped sending us those five nines?"

"Aye, 'nother fine evenin' in te trenches, sir."

"Any signs of the Boche moving around?" Rutledge asked. They had listening posts and snipers waiting for any signs of life.

"Nay, me thinks tey are as tired as we."

"Have the men been fed then?"

"Aye, tey hav. Hunkerin' down fra a wee bit o a rest," Hamish said softly.

"Good, well, let me take a walk along the line and talk to the men."

"An git som rest yerself, sir."

Rutledge made his way up and down the line. From time to time, he would see some men playing cards or chatting softly. Any loud noises would wake the Boche. Neither side wanted that. Stopping from time to time, Rutledge would speak to the men. He tried to sound cheerful and offer encouragement or make some humorous remark. A polite laugh or a "you got that right" was all he was trying to accomplish.

Days went by with not much more excitement. Trench warfare was boredom punctuated by fighting for your life. Eventually, orders came through to Rutledge and replacements came to relieve them. More training in the rear meant the High Command had some new plan. Rutledge would have to write more letters home again.

Rutledge stopped by Captain Murray's sector and bid him farewell for now. On his way back to his men, he stopped to speak to Sergeant Sullivan.

"You keep up the hard work, Sergeant. You are an inspiration for the men."

Rising to attention, Sergeant Sullivan gave Rutledge a formal salute, which Rutledge returned.

With a grin on his face, Sullivan said, "I'll be lookin' for ya at The Devil's Tavern, on the two-year celebration of the end o' this mess. Mark your calendar and come have a drink on me!"

Rutledge shook Sullivan's large hand and promised he would.

LONDON, NOVEMBER 1920

Rutledge had arrived in London after a case in Cornwall and was happy to be back in his rooms. He had completed his reports and submitted them. Chief Superintendent Markum seemed pleased with his verbal recounting of the case. After a long day at work, Rutledge was excited to wash up and change into clean clothes.

It was Thursday the eleventh of November, a day Rutledge had tried to force to the back of his mind. Hamish, on the other hand, had been railing at him all day. Rutledge decided to go out to a local restaurant for an early supper.

Rutledge donned his coat and hat and went downstairs and into the street. It was not the holidays yet, and the streets were silent. The cold air convinced Rutledge that his coat and hat were certainly required.

On this second anniversary of the Armistice, most of the crowds were at The Cenotaph, which had been unveiled today with much pomp and circumstance. Rutledge was grateful his office was well down Whitehall and away from the ceremonies. Over in Westminster Abbey, they had interred the unknown soldier in the Tomb of the Unknown Warrior today as well. Rutledge shuddered against the cold and his never-ending memories of the war. He had no need for ceremonies and speeches to remind him of the war he saw with his own eyes.

Turning down the street, he stepped into his local pub and restaurant. Sarah was waiting tables, as she did most nights, and smiled at Rutledge as he removed his hat and coat.

"And what will you be having tonight, Mr. Rutledge? Your usual?"

"Yes, Sarah, and a whiskey if you please. Chilly night out."

"I'll have it right away, sir, and tell the cook what ya ordered," Sarah replied.

"Thank you, Sarah. I hope you are well?"

"That I am, sir. I'll just get your whiskey."

As Sarah left for the bar, Rutledge gazed around the room. It was old and suited him. The high ceiling made of exposed timbers did not crowd him. He tried to avoid the claustrophobic feeling he carried home from the war. It was why Rutledge insisted on driving his car to the various places the Yard sent him. The thought of crowded train stations and small compartments on the train was more than he could bear.

"Ye 'ill be needin te whiskey ta nite. No amount o' whiskey will git rid o' me tho," Hamish said.

Rutledge knew Hamish was dead, and by his own hand no less.

He was used to the voice in his head. It had been there since the summer of 1916, at the height of the Battle of the Somme. It had been the bloodiest of battles, and men died before his eyes, day and night, until the trenches reeked of rotting flesh and black mud and death. He wasn't the only one on the verge of breaking as the Germans had pressed harder and harder, hoping to end the stalemate of 1915.

And then orders had come down to take out a German machine-gun nest that was perfectly situated to halt the next British attack. But it was too well protected, and wave after wave of men had tried and failed to take it. Their wounded and their dead seemed to be piled high around them, and Corporal Hamish MacLeod had finally refused to lead another attack against the machine-gun position. He pointed out what Rutledge had known from the start, that it was hopeless and a waste of good men. But the next attack was coming, and Rutledge was all too aware the slaughter would be unimaginable if the first waves were caught in the open with that gun on their flank.

He had reasoned with Hamish, he had threatened, and it did no good. Hamish was as sick of the killing as he was, and weary of dragging their dying and wounded back to the trench. He had looked at the men who were left, and he had said, "It's murder, pure and simple. I will na' do it anymore. I canna' do it anymore. No man in his right mind can justify it."

And with the next assault only hours away, coming with the dawn, Rutledge had had no choice but to make an example of his corporal before the rest of his men lost heart and refused to follow orders as well. Military necessity. The words still haunted him.

"Yer no celebratin' the armistice then. Afraid they will ken yer a coward?" Hamish said.

"Nothing of the sort, and you know it," Rutledge replied, and then looked around, realizing he had spoken aloud.

No one was looking in his direction, but Sarah was on her way to his table with his whiskey.

Setting his glass on the table, Sarah said, "The cook says ya meal will be right along."

"Thank you, Sarah," Rutledge replied.

Taking a long slow sip of his whiskey, Rutledge leaned back in his chair and let out a deep breath. He knew he needed the rest and yet he was eager for his next assignment.

People came and went, some chatting with the barman and some sitting quietly at their tables. Eventually, Sarah came to the table with his meal.

"Did ya go to The Cenotaph unveiling today?" she asked.

"He war tae scared ta go," Hamish said.

"No, Sarah, I had to work. Did you go?" Rutledge replied.

"Nae, I had to work. Some of the customers said it was a touching ceremony. The King was there as they unveiled the new permanent one. Rather exciting, they said," Sarah replied.

"I will have to go pay it a visit. I assume the attendance was formidable."

"Yes indeed, sir. More to come, or so they say. Well, enjoy your meal, sir," Sarah said before she turned away to check on her other customers.

Rutledge enjoyed his meal. Simple fare was just what he wanted. Rising from his seat, Rutledge placed some coins on the table to cover his meal, then put on his coat and hat and went out onto the street.

The fresh air agreed with Rutledge, and he was in no hurry to go back to his rooms. As he wandered down the street, Rutledge thought about the Tomb of the Unknown Warrior. As Kipling put it, there were so many men who were "Known only to God."

Looking at his watch, Rutledge suddenly thought about Sergeant Sullivan and his promise to his men. "You'll have a drink on me at The Devil's Tavern on the second anniversary of the war's end," Sullivan had said.

Rutledge's company had rotated out of the front trench not long after Sullivan had joined the company next to his. Sullivan was a good noncommissioned officer and worked well with his men. Rutledge had always wondered whether Sullivan would survive the war and be able to buy his men some drinks.

The more he walked, the more Rutledge was curious about what had happened to Sullivan and his men. He knew The Devil's Tavern from his time on foot patrol. He had worked every rung of the ladder at the Yard, although some were still jealous he had risen so fast.

The Devil's Tavern was in fact The Prospect of Whitby located down the Thames in Wapping. It was near the old ports and had a reputation in the past that lived up to its Devil's Tavern moniker.

Looking up and down the street, Rutledge spied a hackney coming in his direction and hailed the driver down. Stepping into the rear of the cab, he gave the driver the address.

"Whut would a gentleman like yourself want wi' that place?" the driver said sourly.

"Mind your driving, and leave my business to me," Rutledge replied firmly.

That ended the conversation, and from there they rode in silence.

After a bit, the hackney pulled up at the tavern and Rutledge got down. After paying his fare, the driver touched his cap and was off about his business.

From the street, Rutledge could hear a raucous crowd in the tavern. Not much had changed with the years.

Rutledge stepped through the door and took off his hat and coat. A wary crowd fell silent for a moment and then returned to their frivolity.

Rutledge made his way to the bar and, after a few minutes, got the attention of the barman.

"I'll have a whiskey," Rutledge told the man.

Nodding, the barman went to his shelves and grabbed a glass. Setting it on the bar mat, he poured the whiskey into the glass. When he was finished, Rutledge laid some coins on the bar and invited the barman to join him.

"Mebbie later, but thank ya just the same," the barman replied as he put a whiskey's worth of coins in a jar behind the bar and rang up the rest.

As he handed the change to Rutledge, Rutledge asked, "I was wondering if any of Sergeant Sullivan's men made it here tonight."

"Yes, they are in the back room just there," the barman said, gesturing to a hallway.

Rutledge thanked the barman and headed toward the back room.

There were about fifteen men gathered in the room. Rutledge looked about for Sullivan but did not see him in the crowd.

Suddenly, a voice came from the other side of the room. "Why, it is Captain Rutledge, if my eyes don't deceive me."

The group of men fell silent and looked at Rutledge.

"I . . . I happened to remember Sergeant Sullivan today and thought I would come by," Rutledge stammered.

The owner of the voice came toward Rutledge, finally reaching him. "Ya were the captain o' the next company over from us when we attacked that Boche trench for a prisoner. Corporal Smithers, sir. I was a private then."

"Well, Smithers, I am glad to see you made it home. What became of Sullivan?"

"Come over har and I'll explain." Taking Rutledge by the elbow, Smithers led him to a corner of the room. There on a small table was a photograph of Sergeant Sullivan with the top of the frame draped in black.

"Sadly, sir, he did not make it home. It was the Somme that got him, sir."

"So you all got together anyway to toast his memory?"

"More than that. Ya see, he sent part o' his wages home to the tavern here so we could have a drink on him tonight. He had no family, so his pay was just for his needs and the drinks for his men who made it back."

"God bless the man; he was one of a kind," Rutledge said softly.

"That he was, sir," Smithers replied, and turned to the men in the room.

"All right, lads, let's raise a glass to Sergeant Sullivan. Three cheers for the sergeant!

"Hip, hip, hooray . . ."

WARD LARSEN

WHAT DO YOU DO FOR MONEY HONEY

"Blond at the end of the bar, bad facelift and a double vodka."

Thomas Driscoll shimmied onto a high stool next to Burt Torkelson. He didn't venture a look down the bar. Not yet. A Fat Tire was waiting for him on a cocktail napkin, enough beaded sweat to suggest it had been there a while.

Having to focus on something, he looked at Torkelson. Driscoll saw what he always saw. A grizzled fiftysomething ex-cop, thirty extra pounds in all the wrong places. Cheeks, gut, turkey-wattle neck. He was wearing what was practically a uniform, loose chinos and an oversized short-sleeve shirt left untucked—concealed-carry chic. In the five years Torkelson had been working for him, his look never varied.

Driscoll picked up the beer, only because it would have been odd not to. He wasn't supposed to be drinking—doctor's orders—so he took only a brief sip. The beer was room temperature.

"How long has she been here?" Driscoll asked.

"Got here at three fifty-eight. Happy hour started at four."

"And she comes every day?"

"I've only been watching her since yesterday, but so far she's two-for-two."

Driscoll had never been to this bar, but he'd seen plenty like it. Scored wood and bottom-shelf liquor, the tang of stale beer and sweat riding the air. He'd haunted his share of such dives in college and graduate school, but that had been twenty years ago. These days he was more accustomed to high-end wine bars and elite private clubs.

Driscoll took a second swig, gummed up his courage, and glanced down the length of the L-shaped bar. He saw her at the far end, framed between a tattooed longshoreman-type and a jukebox that belonged in a time capsule. She was holding the vodka with both hands, almost reverently. An empty tumbler sat next to it. Her hair was straight from a bottle, and while her face did seem taut at the edges, Driscoll thought her attractive in a vampish kind of way. Her red blouse showed some cleavage, although not enough to qualify as trashy. She wore heavy makeup, and her lips were artificially puffy. She was clearly alone, one empty stool between her and the longshoreman. She studied her drink like it held the secret to the universe.

When her eyes canted suddenly upward, Driscoll turned toward Torkelson.

"Her name is Marcia Dahl," Torkelson said.

"Do you know where she lives?" he asked.

"Wouldn't be much of a PI if I couldn't find out things like that. Fifties ranch-style in Milpitas, fifteen hundred square feet. Needs a new roof and serious refinancing. It's all in the file." Torkelson reached for a leather portfolio on the empty stool next to him.

"No, not here," Driscoll said. "We'll go over it tomorrow morning. Come to my house, eleven."

"All right," Torkelson said, leaving the portfolio where it was.

"How did you find her?" Driscoll asked.

"You're not the only one who has a way with technology. I've got contacts, but I'd rather not divulge them."

Driscoll studied him for a moment but didn't respond. He'd had Torkelson on retainer for five years, an all-purpose gladiator to engage the complications that came with being one of the most successful tech moguls on earth. Extortion scams, sketchy venture capital schemes, baseless lawsuits. There was nothing like being a NASDAQ celebrity to put a bull's-eye on one's back. For Torkelson, tamping down Driscoll's problems had become a full-time gig.

Today's job was three months in the making and had been instigated by an offhand suggestion from Torkelson. As a kind of insurance, he had floated the idea of Driscoll having a DNA profile run by an up-and-coming genealogy company. Torkelson explained that the results would make it easier to swat down paternity lawsuits, of which Driscoll had battled a few, along with other potential legal entanglements. After ruminating on the idea for a few days, and researching the company carefully, Driscoll decided to do it. He sent off a saliva sample, and the results arrived three weeks later. The genealogy turned out much as he'd expected. He was mostly German, with some Eastern European thrown in. Two percent Neanderthal. Yet there were two asterisks in the report that had nothing to do with his ancestry. The first, which Torkelson knew nothing about, had precipitated a doctor's appointment. The second was sitting at the far end of the bar.

"I might see a resemblance," Torkelson ventured. "The nose, the line of her jaw."

"Your observational prowess aside, I deal only in science."

"I'd say you've got that."

Torkelson had a point. The Helix report had included a paragraph at the end explaining that crosschecks of its database had gotten one hit: another customer's DNA shared an unusually high commonality with his own.

"What was the number again?" Torkelson asked.

"Almost a twenty-five percent match."

He again looked at the woman. "Yeah, I can see it. And that's a sibling?"

"A half-sibling."

The detective shifted in his chair. "But you never had any brothers or sisters."

"None that I know about. It seems one of my parents had a little secret. Since Marcia is three years older than I am, she would have been born before they got married."

"Sounds complicated. But as a detective, I can tell you, things like that happen."

"If I'd found out about this before my parents passed away, I would have confronted them. As it is . . ."

"Did you consider going through Helix to get her name?"

"They offered that option, for a nominal additional fee. But playing by the rules seemed problematic. They only allow an exchange of names with the consent of both parties. I need to know what I'm getting into before Marcia learns my name."

Torkelson nodded sympathetically. "That much I get. Telling someone, out of the blue, that they're related to one of the richest men in the world does invite complications."

"The kind of complications you and I know a lot about. But there was another, more pressing reason. If I had simply authorized Helix to share my name, hoping that my half sister would be similarly inclined— it would have taken the best part of a month."

"And that's a problem?"

Driscoll dodged the question by changing the subject. "I *am* impressed you found her. All you had to work with was the deidentified case number in the Helix report. If I was a detective, I might suspect you had a source inside the company."

"Like I said, I'd rather not get into it. Just trust me when I say, my information is solid."

"All right. I'll take your word for it."

Torkelson rubbed the label on his bottle. "So the bottom line is that Marcia Dahl may be your sister."

"Very possibly."

"What are you going to do about it?"

"I haven't decided. To begin, I want to hear what's in your report. My own circumstances also have a bearing on where this leads."

"Circumstances?"

"I have an appointment tomorrow morning that might guide my thinking."

Torkelson regarded him closely. "Would that be a doctor's appointment?"

Driscoll frowned but didn't deny it.

His investigator studied him. "Not exactly my business, but you've been having a lot of those lately."

"You're right—it's none of your business. Not yet, anyway." Driscoll glanced again at the blond. She was talking to the bartender, their rapport casual, familiar. He felt Torkelson's eyes on him as he watched her.

"Is she what you expected?" the investigator asked.

"I'm not sure what I expected. But it's good to have a face to go with . . . whatever you're going to tell me tomorrow."

"You want me to keep an eye on her tonight?"

"No, that won't be necessary." Driscoll hesitated before adding, "Although there is one thing that might be helpful." He explained what he wanted, then watched Torkelson as he considered it—both the act and its implications.

"I suppose you can never be too careful. It shouldn't be a problem."

"Tomorrow we'll discuss further steps."

The ex-policeman looked at him squarely, appraisingly, yet he didn't ask the obvious question. Driscoll knew he was beginning to look rough. His features were weighted and strained, his weariness evident. His complexion had taken on a claylike pallor. A month ago he'd quit surfing, and he'd barely seen the sun all week. He was becoming a shadow of his typically vibrant, outdoors self.

A flurry of movement at the end of the bar drew their attention. The longshoreman had shifted over one stool and was trying to strike up a conversation with Marcia. She never even looked at him, her expression saying, *pound sand.*

"I wonder why she comes here," Driscoll pondered aloud.

"My report tomorrow might shed some light on that."

"Good," Driscoll said, pushing away his half-full Fat Tire. "I'll see you then."

Torkelson watched his employer disappear out the front door.

He waited.

He was midway through his second slowly nursed beer, twenty minutes later, when Marcia Dahl dropped a wad of crumpled bills on the bar. He watched her get up and head for the door, her curvaceous figure amplified as she moved. The practiced sway of a woman who turned heads and knew it.

When she disappeared, Torkelson allowed a grin.

Having already settled his tab, he moved quickly. He picked up his portfolio with one hand, his nearly empty mug with the other, and circled to the far end of the bar. He paused abeam the seat Marcia had been occupying, placed his portfolio on the stool, and set his mug on the bar beside her empty tumbler. Torkelson went to the jukebox and let his eyes run down a playlist straight from the eighties. He dropped in a few coins he carried for various scams—who *used* real money anymore?—and selected the perfect track. The tune began playing.

You're working in bars, riding in cars
Never gonna give it for free . . .

When Torkelson turned back to the bar, he gauged the scene at a glance. The bartender was busy cleaning a spill with a towel. The rebuked longshoreman had engaged his neighbor on the opposite side and was grousing about union politics. Torkelson drained his beer, set the mug back on the bar, and retrieved his portfolio. He turned away and walked to the bathroom. Only an astute observer would have noticed what had gone missing.

Two minutes later, with his portfolio tucked under one arm and a newly empty bladder, Torkelson strode outside into the warm afternoon sun.

Wealthy people often utilize concierge physicians. Fabulously wealthy people enjoy a private health-care system all their own. Which was why, at eight o'clock sharp the next morning, Dr. Linda Silver was waiting patiently in her office when Driscoll arrived.

"Good morning, Thomas," she said.

"Good morning, Linda."

The two took their respective seats, the oncologist behind her weighty desk, the patient in a very comfortable opposing chair. The computer monitor on her L-shaped workstation was booted up and ready.

"Can I offer you some tea?" she said.

"No," Driscoll replied in a clipped tone. "Let's just get on with it."

"Of course."

The doctor opened a file on the computer, the screen already angled so both of them could see it. "I have the results from your latest workup." She met his gaze with a practiced expression. "I'm afraid it's not what we were hoping for. The numbers from your liver, kidney, and bone marrow functions are all worrisome. You also have highly elevated tumor-marker levels."

Silver pulled up an image on the monitor. "This is the latest CT scan. As you can see, the shadows have gotten larger, particularly the one on your left lung."

She directed his attention to points of concern, her tone dry and clinical. Driscoll barely looked at the screen.

When she seemed done, he had but one question. "Options?"

"I have to be frank, Thomas. In spite of our best efforts, the disease is spreading rapidly. There are precious few courses for treating pancreatic cancer, particularly at this advanced stage."

Driscoll waited, expecting a Hail Mary option to be presented. It didn't come. "So that's it?" he asked in a hollow voice. "There's nothing we can do?"

"You told me at the outset that you wanted the truth, no matter how difficult it might be. There is a radical surgical procedure, but the long-term survival rates are extremely poor. The fact that your cancer has already spread to other organs further lessens the chance of success. There are alternative-medicine therapies, but none have a promising track record."

Driscoll's face collapsed to a mask of resignation. None of this came as a surprise, not really. Dr. Silver *had* been straight with him from the outset when the first scans showed an ominous dark shadow. Yet what she was telling him now sounded acutely . . . hopeless. Little time remained for what he had to do.

"How long?" he asked, his voice cracking.

"It's always difficult to say in such—"

"How long, for Christ's sake?"

Dr. Silver recalibrated, then said, "Two months, possibly three. Debilitating complications will arise in half that time." She continued for ten minutes, describing the dismal progression that could be expected. Driscoll heard little of it, his thoughts drifting miles away.

Four weeks? Six? Time was achingly short.

He walked out of the office twenty minutes later, oblivious to the world around him. A worker in the office had called his name as he passed the front desk, something about a follow-up appointment next month. *Apparently, she didn't get the word*, he thought scathingly. He approached his Tesla, and the doors unlocked. Moments later, Driscoll was rocketing out of the medical-complex parking lot at a categorically unsafe speed.

"Her maiden name is Burns," Torkelson said, reading from his file.

Driscoll was seated behind the desk in his home office, his hands steepled thoughtfully in front of him. Almost as if praying. The smell of coffee was thick, and bright morning sun sprayed in through the great window behind.

Driscoll regarded a photo of the woman on his desk—it looked like it had been spit out from a dot-matrix printer. He was, after five years, well acquainted with Torkelson's quirks. The fact that his work product came exclusively in hard copy was surely attributable to his years on the police force. Case files, even in this day in age, even in Santa Clara County, were still done the old-fashioned way. For Driscoll, of course, it was a departure of the highest order. He was the majority owner of three technology giants, including the world's newest and brightest social-media platform. Because of it, he was on most days inundated by emails and PowerPoint presentations. In truth, he rather enjoyed Torkelson's printouts and paper clips. They lent a degree of separation between the battles fought here and those encountered at his corporate office. Secondarily, Driscoll, like few men on earth, understood the vulnerabilities of electronic files. The work Torkelson performed for him, invariably, was best left to the digital shadows.

"Forty-six years old," Torkelson continued, flicking to a new page. "Born in Petaluma, the only child of a single mother who worked as a paralegal. Father was never in the picture, not even listed on the birth certificate."

He paused there, letting the implication sink in. If there was a family tie to Driscoll, it was likely paternal.

Torkelson pressed on. "She attended UC Davis for three years and almost graduated. Then her mother had a stroke, and she quit to take care of her. Mom passed away two years later, complications from the original event. There wasn't much to inherit, and Marcia worked in various office jobs afterward. Receptionist at a dentist's office, scheduler for a trucking company. Also did some phone sales. By all accounts, she was a solid employee. Smart and reliable. She's currently working thirty hours a week in a data-entry job. Most of her current problems stem from her marriage. She recently filed for divorce from her husband of twelve years. Vincent Dahl is a sales rep for a fastener company."

Torkelson slid another photo across the desk. Driscoll saw a face like a mugshot, all dark features and furrows. "Fasteners?" he queried.

"Rivets and screws, that kind of thing. All of it comes from China, and Vince handles sales for a three-state territory—California, Oregon, and Nevada. Sells to various industrial manufacturers. He's been with the company for eight years, and before that had the same gig with a smaller distributor. The two filed for divorce three months ago, but it hasn't finalized. Based on the financials I was able to gather—don't ask how—the couple is in a pretty deep financial hole. They bought too much house at the top of the market and are way behind on the mortgage. Vince spends a lot of time in Vegas—ostensibly for work, but he's heavy into sports betting. The divorce petition also mentions infidelity. The marital net worth is underwater and sinking fast."

"Children?" Driscoll asked.

"None." Torkelson went on for another ten minutes. The picture he drew was one of a mostly responsible woman trying to escape a sinking marriage. Marcia was clearly feeling the stress, as evidenced by her barhopping, but so far hadn't fallen off any notable behavioral cliffs.

Torkelson finally looked up from his file. "That's the basics."

Driscoll leaned back in his chair, and after a thoughtful moment, he asked, "Were you able to get what I asked for?"

Torkelson reached into the backpack he'd brought and pulled out a Ziploc bag containing one glass tumbler. He set it on the desk.

Driscoll regarded it curiously. He saw lipstick smudges on the rim. "Is there enough DNA on it to do a profile?"

"Most likely," Torkelson replied, clearly having expected the question.

"Then let's do it."

"I'll send it off this afternoon."

"Will you use Helix again?" Driscoll queried.

"They're the best in the business."

Driscoll pursed his lips but didn't argue the point.

Torkelson said, "Boss, I'm happy to look into this woman's background. And grabbing a sample of her DNA was no biggie. From the looks of it, you may have stumbled onto a long-lost half sister. But I sense there's more going on here."

Driscoll pushed away from his desk. He stood gingerly and ended up leaning on the back of his chair. He looked at Torkelson for a long moment, before saying, "I'm ill, Burt. Very ill."

Torkelson nodded but didn't respond.

"You don't look surprised."

"I wouldn't be much of a detective if I hadn't noticed. How serious is it?"

"As serious as it gets. Ironically, I only learned about it because of that DNA profile. In addition to the genealogy, Helix maps out genetic markers that indicate risks for certain diseases. In my case, there was a sequence suggesting the potential for an aggressive type of cancer. I mentioned this to my primary care doctor, and he ordered some tests. A few anomalies in my bloodwork turned into a full-blown crisis."

Driscoll went to his desk and from the top drawer pulled out a file folder. He opened it, removed a few printed images—glossy paper that Torkelson would appreciate—and set them on the desk.

"The scans show multiple large tumors, and the disease is spreading. Of course, I would have learned about this by now in any event. The report from Helix only brought it to light sooner."

"Jeez," Torkelson remarked. "I'm really sorry, boss. What kind of treatment are they recommending?"

"There was some talk of chemotherapy or radical surgery. Unfortunately, the disease has reached a point where neither has any real chance of success. The bottom line: my cancer is terminal. I've come to terms with that."

Torkelson's tone was flat as he looked over the scans. "I knew you were under the weather, but I never figured it for something so serious. A guy like you, at the top of your game . . . it doesn't seem fair."

"I've done a lot of reflecting in recent weeks. When we're young, we all think we're bulletproof. Then age creeps in, little things start to go wrong. This disease is robbing me of a good many years, and I went through a full spectrum of emotions after my diagnosis. The usual denial and anger. When the dust settled, I found myself thinking about life in an all-new way."

Driscoll meandered to the wide window that overlooked the sculpted grounds of his mansion. The pathways and gardens were laid out with a perfectionist's eye. "As you know, I've never married or had children. My parents are dead, and I have no siblings—or so I thought until recently. My companion has always been my work, and I've been fortunate there. Over the last twenty years, I've achieved a level of success few men ever see. But now? Now I've been hit with the bleakest news a person can get. I can tell you, it gives one an entirely new perspective."

"And this is where Marcia Dahl comes in?"

"Yes."

Torkelson turned pensive. "Given what you're telling me, new perspectives and all . . . what's the plan if it turns out that she is your sister?"

"I'm going to see my lawyer tomorrow and instruct him to draw up a provisional will. As you know, I was planning to leave my estate, in its entirety, to a handful of charities."

Torkelson did know this—he had been tasked to research a number of organizations last year to weed out unworthy causes.

"If Marcia turns out to be my sister," Driscoll continued, "I'll sign a new document that leaves everything to her. The concept of actually having family, of leaving a blood legacy—I suddenly find it very appealing. By your own report, Marcia has fallen on hard times. Yet she's never shied away from work, and there have long been flashes of ambition. I'd like to think that's a genetic predisposition. Given the chance, I think Marcia might prove a good steward of my empire."

Torkelson nodded slowly. "Could be. But tell me one thing. Those charities that are the beneficiaries in your will now—are they aware of your existing plans?"

"They are not. I always expected a longer horizon, and I assumed that over time the names on the list would change. The selected organizations were to learn of my largesse only after my passing."

"That's good," Torkelson said. "Because if they *did* know, they might make legal challenges to a last-minute change of your will."

"That won't be an issue. If this final DNA test matches, I'll be convinced. It's the closest thing to a bloodline I could ever expect. I would want to meet Marcia, of course, but I'm sure we could come to an accord. She needs a mission in life, and I need someone capable of continuing what I've built."

Torkelson stood and retrieved the tumbler from the desk. "Okay. I should be able to get expedited results in a couple of days."

"The sooner, the better."

The two men shook hands, and as they did Driscoll took on a look of uncertainty.

"Something bothering you?" Torkelson asked.

"While this test is run, it does give a window for . . . reassurance.

Marcia seems to have gone a bit off the rails lately. The drinking, her impending divorce. I would like to be sure of her character."

"How can I help?"

Driscoll tapped the fingers of one hand on his desk, a piano player warming up. "Perhaps you could keep an eye on her for a day or two, until we get a definitive answer."

"Sure, boss. Anything to help."

Torkelson parked three houses away from Marcia Dahl's residence. What he saw in the driveway surprised him, but only mildly. Vince Dahl's leased Mercedes was there, the trunk lid open and one rear door ajar. He presumed it was Vince's car based on the DMV records in his file. He was sure of it when Vince himself, in all his slick-salesman glory, came strutting out the front door with an armload of boxes. He dropped them unceremoniously into his car.

The divorce was running full steam ahead.

Twenty minutes later, the Mercedes was loaded—Vince had to sit on the trunk to get it closed, and a kayak paddle poked up through the sunroof like a periscope. Marcia was at the portico, and Torkelson saw, but could not hear, a terse exchange across the driveway. It was the kind of scene he'd seen countless times, both as a cop and a private investigator. Bad vibes as thick as fog as a marriage went down in flames. Conversely, he knew that as soon as Vince drove out of sight, both husband and wife would feel a measure of relief. Even a trace of anticipation for what the future might hold.

And for Marcia Dahl, the future held a lot.

That was exactly how it played out. As soon as the Mercedes was gone, disappearing like a suburban submarine, Marcia seemed to relax. She checked the mailbox and plucked a few flowers from a gardenia bush. She even gave a cordial wave to the yard guy across the street as he loaded up his lawn mower.

Then she went inside.

Torkelson waited ten minutes to make his next move. He wanted to be sure Vince didn't come back for something he'd forgotten.

When he was satisfied, he got out, locked his car silently with the key, and strolled toward a three-two ranch, in a good school district, that would soon be hitting the market. When he reached the driveway, he checked discreetly in both directions, then veered toward a gate on the east side of the garage. Torkelson already knew there was no dog. He saw a yard sign for a security company but knew that the monitoring had gone inactive due to nonpayment—always one of the first things to go for couples on the brink of financial ruin.

Moments later, he was in the backyard. Keeping his back to the wall, he edged toward the big sliding window that overlooked the kitchen. He saw Marcia working at the stove. The counters around her were shambolic, the sink a shipwreck of dirty dishes. With practiced silence, Torkelson went to the slider, eased it open, and approached her from behind.

When he was two steps away, with the song from the jukebox stuck in his head, he said, "What do you do for money, honey?"

She whipped around, a Rubbermaid spatula brandished over her head.

"Christ!" she said. "You scared the crap out of me!"

Torkelson smiled. He moved closer, until their hips engaged, then pulled her in for a kiss. When it broke, he inquired, "How long will Vince be gone?"

"Not long enough for what you have in mind." She shoved him away. "Why can't you just ring the doorbell like a normal person?"

"Because we can't be seen together. At least, not yet."

The spatula smacked his hip. "I'm making an omelet. You want one?"

"No," he said. Marcia was a looker, but she was a lousy cook.

She began breaking eggs into a bowl, bits of shell falling in. "How did the meeting with Driscoll go?"

"Like a dream." He pulled the tumbler from his pocket and showed it to her.

She recognized it instantly. "You grabbed that from the bar?"

"Boss's orders."

"What are you going to do with it?"

Torkelson dropped it into the trash can on top of the eggshells. "Make sure you take out the garbage this week."

"Are things happening that fast?"

"They are—and at this point, we can't afford any mistakes."

"Should I keep going to the bar?"

"Nah. Driscoll just needed to see you once—a convincing face to go with the rest."

"And was I? Convincing?"

"You played it perfect."

"So what's next?"

"We got some big breaks today. When he asked me to grab that tumbler, I knew he wanted a second DNA test. I was afraid he was going to insist on a different lab, but when I suggested using Helix again, he didn't flinch."

Marcia smiled. "That makes it easy." And truly it did. Marcia had been working in the operations division of Helix Labs for six months now. She had altered Driscoll's genealogy report to include the paragraph about the possible sibling, and also manipulated her own profile to create a match. It would be simplicity itself to copy and paste one last report from a blank template—one that showed just the right amount of common DNA.

"That's not the best part," he said. "He finally told me about his illness."

She looked at him expectantly. They knew Driscoll wasn't well, but the exact nature of his malady had escaped them.

"Turns out he's got cancer. He actually discovered it because of that original report from Helix."

"The health-risk markers at the end?"

"Yep."

"But those weren't real. I just made them up so he'd worry a little about his future, think about changing his will."

"Yeah, I know. But when he saw that he was high risk for some things, he got his doctor to run tests. Turns out, he's terminally ill. Only got a couple of months to live."

Marcia acquired a pained look. "That's awful. Poor guy."

"Hey, we all end up there someday. And you have to admit, the timing couldn't be better for us. Driscoll is set to talk with his lawyer tomorrow. If this test on the tumbler seals the deal, he's going to change his will. In a few months, you're gonna be a very wealthy woman."

"What if some judge figures out I'm not really his sister?"

"We have DNA reports that prove you are. And anyway, who's gonna ask? There's nobody to contest the will."

A pungent smell filled the air, something on the burner from last night. Marcia turned on the range blower. "It's still sad," she said over the noise.

"Look, Driscoll had a good run. For us it's—What's that word?—*serendipity*. And it saves me from having to create an accident."

Marcia frowned. She had never liked that part. "You really could have killed him? In a way that wouldn't come back at us?"

"I wouldn't be much of a detective if I couldn't do something like that."

Marcia flipped her omelet. Liquid eggs splattered all over the counters and backsplash.

Torkelson walked into Driscoll's home office again two days later. Driscoll was on the phone when he arrived, so he made himself comfortable in his usual chair. The big desk was set up like any weekday, twin monitors fired up with graphs and spreadsheets. A financial channel ran silently on the wall-mounted television. *Some guys work all the way to the grave*, Torkelson thought.

The phone call ended.

"So," Driscoll began, "did you get the results of that test?"

"I did." Torkelson pulled out a lone sheet of paper from his inside jacket pocket—no portfolio necessary—and slid it across the desk. Driscoll picked it up and put it in a desk drawer.

"Aren't you going to look at it?" Torkelson asked.

"No need. I know what it says."

Torkelson cocked his head, but let it go. "So congratulations, you've got a sister. I guess you're gonna make those changes to your will?"

"I did make changes . . . although not quite the ones we discussed. The truth is—" his words were cut off when his phone rang. "Excuse me . . ."

Driscoll took another call, most of which was spent listening. At the end, he said, "It's time then, send out the release. Follow up as we discussed—no mercy." He hung up.

Torkelson tried not to panic about the will. He found himself staring at Driscoll. Something, he realized, was different. He seemed more energetic, less subdued. "You still doing deals, boss? I mean, with all that's going on in your life?"

"I'll be doing deals on my deathbed, Burt." He paused somewhat theatrically, before adding, "But that won't be for some time."

Torkelson looked at him quizzically.

Driscoll said, "A few months ago, when you first floated the idea of doing a DNA profile, I thought you pushed it rather aggressively. Because I own technology companies, people expect me to be a nerd. They think I have one of those brains that understands coding and logic, but with limited social awareness. The truth is, it's quite the opposite. I've always had far less aptitude for technology than I do for human nature. That's how you get *really* rich in Silicon Valley.

"Despite my suspicions about your recommendation, I decided to roll with it. I sent off a DNA sample to Helix, and when the profile came back, I studied it carefully. The genealogy made sense, and I'm guessing it reflected an actual test. The mention of an unknown half-sibling, however—that was a huge red flag. So I did a little investigating of my own, and I learned that the file you gave me on Marcia Dahl was mostly accurate, but with some crucial deviations. The most relevant, of course, is that she and I have no blood relationship whatsoever."

"Now wait a minute," Torkelson broke in. "I don't know where you got—"

"Please, Burt. Let me finish. The more interesting discovery was that Marcia Dahl is actually employed by Helix Labs. She works in the data section and has virtually unlimited access to customer profiles."

Torkelson didn't bother to deny it, and Driscoll could see the wheels turning in his head. Slow as they might be.

Driscoll said, "You, of all people, know that I'm never one to squander an opportunity."

"Opportunity?" Torkelson parroted.

Driscoll looked up at the television. "Ah, here we are."

He raised the volume slightly as the anchor on the business channel announced a breaking news story. The usual roll of stock prices was replaced by a headline: `Whistleblower Accuses Helix Corporation of Customer Data Breach.`

Driscoll let the segment run for thirty seconds, then muted the TV.

"You get the idea," he said. "For a company like Helix, strict confidentiality is not simply a goal—it is essential to their business plan. Without it? Well, that's rather like an airline losing its reputation for flight safety. The very core of such businesses is trust. I have no doubt that Helix will launch a thorough investigation, and it won't be hard to uncover Marcia's duplicity. I expect she'll turn against you. Let me guess—it was your idea for her to apply for the job at Helix?"

Torkelson didn't reply.

"When she does confess, it will become clear that the breach was the work of a single employee, and also that only one client was affected. A client who, for shamelessly self-serving reasons, will not pursue any legal action. In the end, the reputational damage for Helix will prove quite minimal. The key point, however, is that all that takes time."

"What are you playing at?" Torkelson asked.

"I've had my eye on Helix for some time. They really are at the forefront of their market. Today's headlines are sure to bring a swoon in the stock price, and my brokers will buy as fast as they can."

"You're trying to take over Helix?"

"I *will* take over Helix, and at a very attractive price."

"But you're manipulating the stock price. I could take that to the authorities."

"Could you? You're the one who dreamed up this scheme. What have I done, other than submit DNA samples, on your advice, to a seemingly reputable company? It's true that an acquaintance of mine has laid bare a criminal conspiracy inside Helix, but today I'm only doing what all successful businessmen do—taking advantage of a dip in the price of a good long-term investment. I've had many dealings with the SEC, and my lawyers wouldn't break a sweat defending my actions. You, on the other hand, have substantial legal exposure."

Driscoll moved to the great panoramic window and looked outside contemplatively.

Torkelson started to slowly stand.

"Before you do anything you might regret," Driscoll said, obviously seeing the movement in the reflection, "there are a few things you should consider."

Torkelson froze, then eased back into the chair.

"First, when I do gain control of the company, I will have considerable leverage over your legal troubles going forward. As things stand, I wouldn't press for criminal prosecution, nor would I bother with civil suits. Marcia will be let go, of course, and I'll also insist that you seek new employment. At this point, I think we can agree, the trust between us is less than is necessary to continue our association. Beyond that, however, assuming our split remains amicable, I expect we'll both get on with our lives."

"You far wealthier; Marcia and me looking for work."

"I don't see any other outcome. I did consider how you were going to cash in on this scheme, and the only answer that came to mind was quite disturbing. With that in mind, I should explain the changes that I actually *did* make to my will. Instead of leaving my entire estate to an alleged half sister, my attorney has added a codicil to the existing document. In essence, it says that if anything untoward should happen to me, my law firm will notify the authorities of your extortion scam, complete with a few audio recordings I've made of our meetings—including this one."

An overwhelmed Torkelson surveyed the room suspiciously. Then he looked Driscoll up and down. "But . . . I don't get any of this. I thought you were sick."

"That was rather devious on my part. I admit my appearance in recent weeks has become suggestive, which probably incentivized you and Marcia to press ahead. In fact, I feel fine. You've probably forgotten, but one of my recently acquired companies operates the servers for an electronic medical-records platform."

It all came back to Torkelson. "You had me work up files last year on the previous owners."

"There, you do remember. The new CEO I installed was happy to do me a few favors. It's true, I did undergo a battery of scans and bloodwork, but everything turned out fine. The results sent to my doctors, however, were sourced from a far less fortunate soul."

"The scans you showed me the other day."

Driscoll smiled. "Convincing, weren't they? As things stand, I don't plan on seeing any of my doctors for roughly six months."

"Won't they be shocked when you walk in fully recovered?"

"I'll have a story by then. Something about an alternative-medicine therapy. Or perhaps I'll be healed by religion. The doctors will be perplexed by my miraculous recovery, but they'll also be happy to have a 'platinum-care' patient back on their books. And here again, what have I done but tinker with my own medical records, which were seen only by my doctors? It's a crime without a victim."

Driscoll turned and faced the television. He smiled at the numbers on the screen.

A perplexed Torkelson stood. Shoulders drooping, he headed silently for the door.

"And by the way, Burt," Driscoll said as Torkelson reached for the handle. "In spite of your opinion otherwise . . . you're really not much of a detective."

ABOUT THE AUTHORS

RICK BLEIWEISS has been a successful musician, songwriter, music producer, and record company executive. He has worked as a social activist and journalist and is currently a publishing executive. His novel *Pignon Scorbion & the Barbershop Detectives* was selected as an Amazon Editors' Pick for Best Mystery, Thriller, and Suspense, as well as being chosen as one of the year's Best New Debut Mystery Novels by *Publishers Weekly*. Rick lives in Gig Harbor, Washington, and is at work on his next Pignon Scorbion novel. Follow him and Scorbion at RickBleiweiss.com.

DON BRUNS is the author of fifteen novels and three series. His New Orleans homicide/voodoo series *Casting Bones* was optioned for television. Bruns's former life as a nightclub performer and world traveler and his South Florida residency has given him a rich background to draw from. Bruns is the editor of five anthologies and the contributor to many others.

ANDREW CHILD was born in Birmingham, England, in May 1968. He went to school in St. Albans, Hertfordshire, and later attended the University of Sheffield where he studied English literature and drama.

After graduation, Andrew set up and ran a small independent theater company which showcased a range of original material to local, regional, and national audiences. Following a critically successful but financially challenging appearance at the Edinburgh Fringe Festival, Andrew moved into the telecommunications industry as a "temporary" solution to a short-term cash crisis. Fifteen years later, after carrying out a variety of roles including several which were covered by the UK's Official Secrets Act, Andrew became the victim/beneficiary of a widespread redundancy program. Freed once again from the straight jacket of corporate life, he took the opportunity to answer the question, what if?

DAVE BRUNS took advantage of the covid pandemic to begin a second career as a writer. Thirty-six years spent working in child welfare prepared him for a walk of life as a storyteller. His clients included drug dealers, smugglers, and murderers, and his Carl Boyd series reflects that experience. Bruns lives in Toledo, Ohio, with his wife, LouAnn Frey, and an obnoxious Portuguese water dog named Roscoe. Look for Bruns's debut novel, *Rule Number Four*, in summer of 2024.

TORI ELDRIDGE is the author of *The Ninja's Oath*, book four in the Lily Wong thriller series—nominated for the Anthony, Lefty, and Macavity Awards, winner of the 2021 Crimson Scribe Best Book of the Year—and the Brazilian dark fantasy *Dance among the Flames*. Her shorter works appear in numerous anthologies. A former actress, singer, and dancer on Broadway, television, and film, Tori holds a fifth-degree black belt in To-Shin Do ninja martial arts. Visit her at ToriEldridge.com.

SANDRA BALZO built an impressive career as a public relations consultant before authoring the successful Maggy Thorsen coffeehouse mysteries, the first of which, *Uncommon Grounds*, was published to stellar reviews and nominated for an Anthony and Macavity Award. She is also the author of the Main Street Murders mystery series.

REED FARREL COLEMAN, called a hard-boiled poet by NPR's Maureen Corrigan, is the *New York Times* bestselling author of thirty-three novels, including six in Robert B. Parker's Jesse Stone series. He is a four-time recipient of the Shamus Award and a four-time Edgar Award nominee in three different categories. He has also won the Audie, Scribe, Macavity, Barry, and Anthony awards. Reed lives with his wife on Long Island.

HEATHER GRAHAM, a *USA Today* bestselling author, has written more than a hundred novels. She has won the Thriller Writers' Silver Bullet Award and a Lifetime Achievement Award from Romance Writers of America. She is an active member of International Thriller Writers and Mystery Writers of America.

CHARLES TODD is a pen name used by the American authors Caroline (1934–2021) and Charles Todd, a mother-and-son writing team who write the Inspector Ian Rutledge mysteries and the Bess Crawford mysteries, as well as stand-alone novels. Their novel *Proof of Guilt* was a *New York Times* bestseller, and *A Test of Wills* was named one of the Independent Mystery Booksellers Association's 100 favorite mysteries of the 20th Century and was a *New York Times* Notable Book of the Year. Their novels have won the Agatha Award, the Barry Award, and the Anthony Award, as well as being finalists for several other awards. Charles is continuing the series.

WARD LARSEN is a *USA Today* bestselling author and seven-time winner of the Florida Book Award. His work has been nominated for both the Edgar and Macavity Awards. He is a former US Air Force fighter pilot who flew combat in Operation Desert Storm. He also served as a federal law enforcement officer and is a trained aircraft accident investigator.